DAVID OWEN was born in Zimbabwe and grew up in Malawi, Swaziland and South Africa. He lived in London before migrating to Australia in 1986. A past editor of *Island* magazine, he writes fiction and nonfiction. He lives in Hobart, Tasmania.

A PUFFERFISH MYSTERY

No Weather for a
Burial

DAVID OWEN

EER
Edward Everett Root, Publishers, Brighton, 2024.

EER CRIME FICTION
Edward Everett Root, Publishers, Co. Ltd.,
Atlas Chambers, 33 West Street, Brighton, Sussex, BN1 2RE, England.
Full details of our stock-holding overseas agents in America, Australia, China,
Europe and Japan, and how to order our books, are given on our website.
www.eerpublishing.com

edwardeverettroot@yahoo.co.uk

We stand with Ukraine!
EER books are **NOT** available for sale in Russia or Belarus.

ISBN: 9781915115478 Hardback
ISBN: 9781915115485 Paperback

This edition © Edward Everett Root Publishers Co. Ltd., 2024.

First published by Forty Degrees South Pty. Ltd, Hobart, Tasmania 2011.

Cover by Hilton Owen.
'Pufferfish' series logo by Hilton Owen.
Cover image: Fluted Cliffs, South Coast
Photographer: Martin Hawes

British production by Pageset Ltd., High Wycombe, Buckinghamshire.

|

THERE'S NOTHING LIKE A BIT OF LONG SERVICE LEAVE TO PUT THE PIPS back in a Detective Inspector's core.

Heineken here. Detective Inspector Franz Heineken, aka Pufferfish, longtime scourge of the Apple Isle's villains. I've been sorting out problems in Tasmania for the best part of thirty years. That's plenty of major crime to flow under one man's bridge, yet here I am, burly shoulder to the wheel, almost through another stint of long service leave and wondering what's stopping me from retiring.

The answer lies in the nickname, which they gave me soon after I cut my teeth as a dour young migrant from Rotterdam, an unhurried outsider of few words, hard to get to know, prickly, feeder off detritus in murky shallows, ability to inflate and even explode under severe provocation. Not the best CV if you want to get along with your new *vrienden* of the Tasmanian Police Force, but effective attributes for the job at hand. Outhinking crims. Outwaiting them. Being a dirty bastard when necessary. Being a cop.

That's Pufferfish. A transplanted Dutch plod. But I'm accepted as a Taswegian now. Almost …

Here's the truth. Thirty years ago I killed a man. Why? Because he'd tortured and murdered my fiancée. I was a trainee constable on the hard Rotterdam waterfront. She was killed because of me, an upstart young cop sniffing around a drug gang. My colleagues arranged it so that the man I shot in cold blood appeared to have been done in by one of his own. In return, I had to disappear. The other side of the world seemed as good a place as any to take my grief and crime.

I found a job as a waiter in Brisbane. Late one evening after my shift I fished a pissed bloke out of the Brisbane River. An off duty local cop, about my age. Grif Hunt. I told him my story. Tasmanian-born, he called a mate in Hobart and swung me an interview with the

TPF. The rest is interesting history, not least because six years ago Grif Hunt came back to Tasmania, head-hunted as the island's Chief Commissioner.

In the whole of this wide brown land that so innocently let me in, only Grif and I know that I'm a murderer, and only Grif and I know that I saved his life. It's made for a complex relationship. Mainly, though, we understand one another, as we age.

NOW, WITH JUST A COUPLE OF DAYS LEFT AT MY BEACH SHACK, THE thought of returning to Davey Square in Hobart – HQ of the TPF – is a mixed one. I'm pissed off. Full of vim, yes, yet not as ripe for action as I should be after three months away from the boredom, blood, mayhem and misery of my profession. You'd think that with barely more than half a million souls, no grimy big cities, and breathtaking natural beauty, Tasmania would somehow be crime-lite. But then you'd also have to believe that human nature, when surrounded by water, somehow elevates itself. Fat chance. In her own uncharming way Tassie's as corrupt and sordid as a cop could want. And we attract some nasty blow-ins. Perhaps I was one all those years ago.

Waiting for me is an unfinished case involving a blow-in – a strange one. Its mystery began to unfold soon after I began my leave. A professor of Egyptology, a Pom by the name of Warwick Collins-Bower, settled here with his wife in retirement. Earlier this year he hosted an international conference at Hobart's Wrest Point Conference Centre, where he launched a scathing attack on the keynote speaker, Sir Roy Hume, accusing him of plagiarism. Go Egyptologists, you might say, and may the maddest man win. Sir Roy took the attack badly. Not surprising, given that it was Warwick who had invited him. And no crime in taking something badly. But the day before Sir Roy flew home to England, Mrs Collins-Bower disappeared – possibly on her daily walk along a well-maintained track at Fern Tree, the suburb nestled around the lower slopes of kunanyi aka Mount Wellington, Hobart's wondrously personal mountain, 1271 metres high, named after a gentleman who had nothing to do with it and, like most mountains, benign one day, treacherous the next. So what's happened to her? My offsider Rafe interviewed the wheelchair-bound husband at length, and neighbours and friends. He even flew to England for an apparently fruitless interview with Sir Roy.

My offsider Rafe. Detective Rafe Tredway, with his rugby league neck, imposing presence and blunt manner, will never be the sharpest tack in the tin, but that doesn't mean he's not a smart cop. We've done some good work together. Always up for a beer and a laugh, this side of thirty, on again-off again with his girlfriend, and the one you'd want beside you in a tight situation. For just over a year now he's been mentoring Detective Constable Faye Addison, graduate of the local police academy, and everything my boofheaded main man's not. She's petite, straight 'A's at college, a serious young kid and good for the future of the force. I'm not exactly looking forward to inducting her into the nastier side of the plainclothes caper, but it's the career she wants, and I'd put in a good case for the extra position in Major Crime South.

MY SHACK HAS ITS OWN UNUSUAL HISTORY. BRUNY ISLAND, SOUTH of Hobart and Storm Bay, is, let's face it, really two islands joined by a long thin neck. Not many went there before it became fashionable. Long ago I happened upon a gaggle of cabins south of Adventure Bay, well isolated by mature forest. The place optimistically called itself the Bruny Health Resort and had, as caretaker, a scrawny Aborigine called Willard. Willard and I got on. We were from different universes, but we formed an unlikely bond and we shared a love of fishing, solitude, and reds around the night fire at his shack.

At one point I helped Willard evade a charge of assault concerning the male half of a Scottish backpacking duo who'd overstayed their welcome at his 'resort'. I advised him what to say to the magistrate. It worked. Just as well, because in a suit and tie in a Hobart court he was out of his depth and scared as hell.

Willard told me one day that his place had been deregistered by the Department of Health and was due to be compulsorily acquired as state forest. He wasn't happy. On his behalf I took the matter as high as I could, with bugger all result. But the land was rich in middens and other artefacts, and the Tasmanian United Aboriginal Corporation demanded a transfer of ownership. Back then they had no chance. Willard subsequently sold me his shack at the southern boundary of the resort, with its own miniature beach and a finger of two-strip gravel winding a few kilometres through the forest. When the 'resort' was finally handed over as Aboriginal land in the 1990s, I was deemed the rightful owner of Willard's shack. The finding didn't please the TUAC, which wanted exclusive rights to a rock islet off the beach – a sacred site – and it didn't please the government, which wanted to turn my track into a logging coupe. Pufferfish's attitude?

Because the trees won't fall, the islet can never be disturbed. And so it is that this imported scourge of villains gets a magical hideaway to rest his weary bones; to wash from his eyes with salty sea the blood and guts of his island's foul play.

TWO MORE LONG SERVICE LEAVE SLEEPS. I'M REMINDED OF THIS BY THE sound of a vehicle. The low growl of Hedda's Toyota 4WD somewhere in the gum trees. Detective Sergeant Hedda Andover, Drug Branch. Hedda and I have what you might call a casually intimate relationship. She's come straight from the airport, having been in Sydney working on an interstate drug case with NSW colleagues, and she's staying here tonight. That'll be good, very good. But tomorrow she's off on the morning's first ferry – twelve minutes, Bruny to the mainland – and into work. She said she wants to come here to 'commiserate' with me before my return. A decent gesture. And we can talk shop if anything of interest has happened lately. Internal cop politics. You wouldn't want to know about it.

I wander onto the front 'lawn' and watch the white vehicle poke and bump its way down the snaky drive, orange kayak on the roof rack should she want a paddle. Out she gets. Tall, fit as buggery. Those patrician cheekbones. That Roman nose, the little kink in which isn't a natural feature but a by-product of the fact she's a second dan shukokai karate expert.

'Mate, you look like Robinson Crusoe!' Hedda gives me a warm hug, peck on the cheek. Runs her fingers across the chin last shaved I don't know how long ago. 'And what the hell's this?' She laughs, rubs the gut that's appeared over the top of my tatty cozzie. 'Crays and abalone aren't fattening!'

'Cascade Premium Lager and Valhalla Ice Cream are. How are you?'

'Good. Shit, it's nice to be here again.' She steps away and inhales the scented air. 'Dunno what stinks worse, Sydney CBD or the insides of aeroplanes.' Now she stretches out her long arms and wiggles her fingers in appreciation of this ethereal place hidden at the edge of an island off an island. 'Reckon I should have a swim, Puff?'

'I can recommend it, even though the water'll freeze your tits off.'

'You wouldn't want that, would you?' She laughs, grabs her travelbag from the Toyota. We enter the dim, black, vertical-board shack of three sloping rooms, dunny out the back surrounded by jackjumper holes. We're in the tiny lounge-room. Its four low walls feature the spines of thousands of cheap paperback novels. I've read them all.

'How did you go in Sydney?' I'm watching her change into her faded-pink one-piece cozzie that lives here.

'Too easy. They're so caught up in all that shit with the Revs and Drags that I was given what I wanted, no questions asked. No one to ask the questions!'

'Nice.'

She's referring to a spectacular flare-up between two Sydney-based bikie gangs that has messily implicated her NSW drug branch colleagues, the Revs being the Revolutionaries, the Drags the Dragons, their fierce rivalry a lethal cocktail of turf war, drug trafficking and mutual racial loathing.

I drape my scruffy towel around my neck, hand her a big, fluffy clean one, warm magenta, never been used. She'll need it. The shack with its slanty ceiling is so small that, making for its front door, we bump into each other. Softly. Not for the first time, and it's always amusing. We walk into the pleasant late-winter sunshine, past the low brick-iron barbecue and craypots and onto the sandy path.

'What's the inside story? All I've caught are breathless headlines.'

'Oh, mate, the usual fight for control of the drug trade, though with a twist. The leadership of the Drags set up a meeting with Deng Xien, Mr Heroin himself, who, as you know, is persona non grata in Oz but cheerily comes and goes from his Honkers base with his various aliases that get him straight through customs. They held their meeting at the Drags' annual muster at Maroubra Beach, this to impress Mr H with the sight of a car park full of red-blooded Asian bikies, and, of course, to fudge the meeting within a lawful annual gathering. But the Drug Branch boys knew he'd be there.'

'Who tipped them off?'

'Dunno, fact is no less than two hundred uniforms and plainclothes closed down the muster. So far so good, and they duly nabbed Xien. But while this was going on, a mob of Revs raided the Drags' drug warehouse way off in Sutherland.'

'Ah, while it was lightly guarded.'

'You bet. And while virtually every available cop was otherwise engaged at Maroubra Beach. So. Did someone in Drug Branch tip off the Revs? "Hey, boys, here's your chance. Do the Anglo thing and get one over the slantyeyes?" It looks that way, and that means an internal investigation at the least.'

'Mhm. Messy.'

'Well, three dead Drags guards, god knows how many kilos of smack, coke, ice and what have you unexpectedly flooding the market, our poor colleagues having to process and interview a few hundred angry bikies on both sides, and a Drug Branch officer probably colluding with the Revs, according to my source. Yeah, it's messy alright.'

We've padded onto the squeaky little white beach, my tinny stashed upside down, a stout chain from the prow looped around a rusty stake driven deep into a granite boulder, legacy of the nineteenth century whaling industry. The emerald-green water winks, and the huge boulders framing the sand glisten wet and glint with mica in the sunshine. Hedda's not a believer in the concept of shallow-water squealing. She drops her towel, runs in until the icy water clasps at her knees and dives powerfully. I watch her stroke repeatedly underwater, through a swell, before kicking up off the sand until half her shiny torso's out the water and she's screaming in thrilled agony at the bite of the Southern Ocean.

We swim to the gently sloped rock, haul out like a pair of seals, one slim and agile, the other more blubbery, and lie flat on our backs to thaw in the sun, hands touching. Eyes closed.

'Reckon you could stay here for keeps, Puff?'

'Tempting. Very.'

'Least it's quiet at Davey Square. You'll not be walking back into anything.'

'I wouldn't bet on that.'

A cormorant skims over us, and we hear it skid onto the wooden spar that is all that remains of a whaleboat jetty. Hedda rolls over to look at the bird. I do too, even though this one's a regular visitor. The faded colour of its leg ring tells me it's a wise old bird. The cormorant hangs its wings out to dry.

'You were standing like that in front of the shack.'

'So I was. Actually, mate, Rafe may have got himself into a bit of strife with Walter. So I heard.'

'Oh, fucking great.'

'But nothing serious. I mean I don't even know what it allegedly is. Just, y'know, one of a thousand scraps of goss that pass for conversation at HQ.'

The keen sunshine feels pleasant on my back and legs. Drowsiness seeps from the granite, works its way through me. HQ. Sounds like an alien spaceship from a faraway galaxy.

'Jeez, but this is nice,' she murmurs, flopping a cool arm across my back. 'All I need now is a shag.'

'You've got a cormorant.'

'Ho ho ho, defective inspector. Okay, beers and lunch and then a shag.'

'I'm up for it. Race you back.'

But we're going nowhere just yet. The warmth spreading through our bodies is infectious, time-shifting, the distant wave sets bouncing onto the firm sand marking the edge of an intimate universe.

Walter. The one true bane of my life. Chief Superintendent Walter D'Hayt is my immediate boss. We are profoundly unalike. He's married to a Stepford with three children and the five of them grin inanely from an overlarge, overcoloured framed photograph on – not behind, on – his desk. He barely trod the mean streets, being a new breed of administrator who wormed his way up the corporate ladder with perfectly clean hands. He wears tailored suits, doesn't seem to be aware that he talks in strangle-inducing public service speak. Yes, he knows his job, his role. And, having an odious charm, he has a seat on the media relations committee and is frequently wheeled out to advise his adoring bi-headed public on 'sensitive' matters, including internal TPF tensions, overcrowding in prison, attitudes towards protestors and the like. For me, he's a painful stickler, a goody two shoes – we call him GTS – a supercilious, vainglorious prick. Enough said.

'I'm hungry', Hedda mumbles into the granite.

'Got cold cray, feta, olives, pickles, crackers, more.'

She sits up. Eyes closed, I feel for and hold a slender ankle.

'Mate, I'm starving.'

'No rush. I'm warming up.'

'You've been on leave too long.' She lies on top of me.

'I'm the wrong way round.'

'I can fix that in the shack.'

'Deal.'

A large cray from these parts, a genuine Southern Rock Lobster, retails on the world market for up to $150. By that estimate I've eaten my way through four grand's worth since my leave started. Who wouldn't be a Tassie cop, eh?

We slip back into the sparkling water and head for shore.

UP THERE IN MELBOURNE THEY FEEBLY BOAST ABOUT HAVING FOUR seasons in one day. Down here, in the runway of the Roaring Forties, we have a fifth, and it generally strikes with little warning. Spring, summer, autumn and winter roll into a tight ball and give us a right old spray. Temperatures plummet in minutes, pleasant sunshine becomes icy rain, pelting horizontal on a ferocious gale, and a dump of snow often blocks the Lyell Highway to the west, cutting off half the island. Unfortunately, this is when bushwalkers become disoriented and, with depressing regularity, perish. Usually they are visitors, sometimes inexperienced in the bush, sometimes disbelieving of Tasmania's wildly unpredictable climate. Sometimes both.

It's this kind of fifth season I'm hearing through the forest and looking at now, up in an angry sky. Hedda drove back yesterday. Perhaps I should have gone too. I knew this was coming. So my last night will be spent locked in the shack. Its two doors, angled as they are, bang angrily if not bolted, and if it pisses down, as I expect, the track out will be no fun. Too bad.

I'm sitting on Willard's multiwood bench, being a plank of blackwood on two sawn-off stumps, the backrest a fat slab of huon pine bolted to the blackwood and angled nicely against an ancient bluegum, its trunk cut to take the pine. At my feet, lumpy rivers of green pigface flow across the native coastal grass. The bothersome kelp flies will soon be whipped away by the wind. I'm on the mobile, leaning back against the smooth yellow wood, idly looking at the oystershell slash on the outer palm of my left hand, now healing well. All that seawater.

'Hello?'

'Nora, *hoi*. Franz.'

'Hi, dad!'

'How are you?'

'Really good. Where are you?'

'In my skin ... At the shack.'

'Not still on hols?'

'All but done. How's Freo?'

'Yeah, same. I'm on my lunch break, actually.'

'Guessed you might be.'

'So what's up?'

'Purpose of call? Nothing much. But I was thinking it might be nice to get together again, don't you think? Maybe a few days over Christmas.'

'Yeah, could be ... I won't have much leave, though.'

'I could fly over for a few days.'

'Not sure what Trent and I are doing ...'

'You still supporting him?'

'Dad. It just happens I'm the breadwinner. No one becomes a successful sculptor overnight.'

'Sure. Or you could come to Tassie. I'll chuck in the air fare.'

'For both of us?'

'Hey, Nora, he's your boyfriend not your husband.'

'What's the difference?'

'Never mind. Anyway, have a think.'

'Yeah, I will, I mean it'd be great to catch up with you, mister big bad cop.'

'How's your mother?'

'Dunno. Bitch. Dad, my latte's arriving. '

'So's mine. Off you go then, girl. Think about Christmas.'

'Love you, dad.'

'*Vaarwel.*'

We disconnect. Hello and goodbye in Dutch. The intimate Pufferfish signature to his young Tasmanian-born daughter currently living in WA. She keeps her mother's name, though not her affections. I advised her to do so because her mother comes from seriously wealthy land-owning stock in three Australian states, and there may be a chance that one day Nora will get some of it. From me there'll be cash, and nothing else, because I don't have anything else. Well, there's this shack.

The water-savvy pigface looks twice as warm as the rapidly chilling air. Time to go in. Time to consider how best to spend one last night in paradise before the return to perfidy.

2

DAVEY SQUARE OVERLOOKS ST DAVIDS PARK, SALAMANCA SQUARE, Parliament House and a fair slice of Hobart's waterfront. It's a huge old building, and various levels or sections are periodically renovated. There has been talk for twenty years about the imminent move to – where? All sorts of sites have been suggested, considered, abandoned, for all sorts of reasons. Now, entering the building after my long break, its familiar smells, lights and noises whip me straight back. I might as well not have been away at all. Great. Colleagues flow either side of me. There are hellos, nods, the occasional look of faint surprise: you still work here?

One thing about an old building. The section of the fourth floor where I work, thanks to its proximity to lift shafts and their internal support structures, can't be trashed and rendered open plan. It has a wide corridor flanked by doors, on the other sides of which are offices. Call me old-fashioned, but I like my thick-walled office, with its crap view of a mossy internal wall and the courtyard. My offsiders are across the corridor in their own office. Hedda's one down. Walter's two up. And Grif Hunt perches in his huge corner eyrie on the eighth, the top floor.

I share the lift with a young constable who looks warily at my daggy brown overcoat and browner briefcase, its leather a riot of hairline cracks. I've seen the look many times before. He probably reckons I'm a seedy private detective. Watch your manner son or I'll poke you in the eye with a bait-scented thumb. Then I look in the lift mirror and I reckon he's got a point. My tan, rare in Tasmania at this time of year, looks like dirt, the skin pale where I shaved last night back in my rented South Hobart weatherboard house. So the youngster's eyeballing a bulky old bastard in a bad coat with an expressionless, disturbingly two-toned face.

A bloke from HR bounces in at the third floor. Seeing me, he's all smiles.

'G'day, Franz! Welcome back.'

'Thanks Gerry.' We shake hands. 'How are things?'

'Good, mate, good.' Being a sound personnel man, he says to the youngster, 'James, this is Detective Inspector Franz Heineken. Franz, James Sparrow, last month's intake.'

James Sparrow's eyes widen. I nod. He swallows. Such is my scaly reputation about this place.

'HELLO, YOU TWO.'

I'm standing in the open doorway of their office. Typically, Rafe's leaning back in his chair, boots on his messy desk, hands behind head, yakking away. Faye's sitting neatly at hers, fingers working her keyboard.

'Boss!' He leaps up noisily, all muscular arms and legs.

'Welcome back, boss,' Faye says, rising demurely. I walk in, drop my briefcase on the spare chair, shake their hands, look around the room.

'Got yourself a tan, boss! Any fish left in the sea?' Rafe grins. It's good to see them both.

'I threw the great white sharks back.'

They laugh.

'It's been quite quiet,' Faye says. 'Great for catching up on paperwork.'

I look at Rafe's desk. 'I can see that.'

'Mate, don't you worry, she's all good here. Just the damn Collins-Bower case …'

'We'll talk about that. Nothing else, nothing at all?'

'Nah. Buggered if Collins …'

I hold up a hand. 'Later. How's upstairs?'

Rafe looks at Faye. She says, 'Um … fine, I think.'

'Good. Well, I can tell you that I relaxed. Enjoyed every minute of it. I'll go and see how many thousand emails I've got, then you can give me a full briefing. Ten o'clock, okay?'

'Sure thing.'

We hear my office phone ring through its closed door. 'Sounds like I'm back,' I say, taking up my briefcase.

The room's neat, because I left it that way. Big desk, two guest chairs, coffee percolator in one corner, filing cabinet, bookshelf. And the phone, ringing.

'Heineken.'

'Franz – Walter. Welcome back on board.'

'Hello, Walter. How are you?'

'Good thanks. Pleasant leave?'

'Very pleasant, thanks.'

'Nothing like recharging the batteries.'

'Sure.'

'Bit of fishing?'

'Yes. And I renovated my bathroom, that really put some zing in my Duracells.'

A fractional silence. Then, 'After all these years, I didn't know you were a handyman.'

'Been quiet here. That's good.'

'Apart from the prison breakout.'

'I saw you hosing it down on the news.'

'And apart from Rafe's moronic behaviour.'

'What do you mean, Walter?'

'You don't know? The disgraceful incident in the Three Bells. I've had to put in some damn hard work to avoid the publican pressing charges!'

'Okay, okay. Look, I'll come up?'

'Please do.'

'I'll just talk to Rafe first.'

I disconnect. My door's open. So's theirs.

'*Fafe!* In here!'

They only ever hear this collective name for them when Pufferfish is as close as he can get to being emotional. I sit, hearing scarred chairleg rubbers scraping wildly on parquet. They enter my spiky domain, Rafe first, Faye in perfect silhouette behind his bulk. I point at the two chairs. They sit. I look at my watch.

'I've been back, what, ten minutes, and GTS is already foaming at the mouth. What the F-word is going on?'

Rafe clears his throat. 'Boss, just the usual, believe me, Walter's got his knickers in a twist over nothing.'

'Oh, right, I'll saunter up and advise him of that, shall I? "Walter, Det. Tredway says you've got your knickers in a twist over nothing".'

'Sorry ... okay, look, we all had a bit much too much to drink at the Three Bells last week when we celebrated the lowest major crime quarter in ten years. I mean, wish you'd been there. Anyway, the pub mirror eventually got dinged, couple of bottles, glasses broken, y'know. Stuff like that happens in a pub.'

' "Dinged." Can you translate, Faye?'

She's looking blinkless at me. 'Well, I reckon they'll be wanting to replace it ...' She can't help herself. She glances at Rafe. He frowns a bit.

'And, uhm, boss, somehow word got to Walter that I, y'know, urinated on a fern in a pot plant or something.'

' "Or something"? And what does that mean, you crapped in one as well?'

He attempts a laugh, quickly gives it away. Silence. Until I drum on the desk with fingers. It tells them just how not happy I am. They stare at me, waiting.

'So, Rafe. I'm about to go upstairs. Tell me, did you or did you not, on or about the blah blah blah, do a number one on a fern in the Three Bells?'

'I guess I was a fair bit in my cups but no, that's not … I mean, me slash in a pot plant?'

'Were you there right through, Faye?'

'Yes.'

'Did someone urinate in a pot plant?'

'I … I think I heard about something like that, at one stage.'

'Was it Rafe?'

'Uh, couldn't be sure. But on balance I mean, no, definitely not.'

'Someone who looks like Rafe?'

'Well, there were heaps of us in the pub.'

'Plenty of eyes to recognise shit-for-brains here.'

Rafe looks hurt. Faye's not finished. 'I … I'm not sure if anyone would admit anything like that to Superintendant D'Hayt, actually say Rafe did it …'

Rafe sees his opening. 'Not a cop in this state would dob me in to GTS, not one.'

'Don't count on it.' I stand. 'I'm going up. Imagine if you're lying to me.'

ANOTHER THING ABOUT WALTER IS THAT HE'S PRACTISED IN THE unsavoury art of making a mountain out of a molehill, to borrow one of his phrases. Yet another is his vindictiveness. I enter his sterilised office. He gestures me to sit. I sit. The framed five grin at me. Walter doesn't.

'So. Presumably Tredway's denying it,' he says.

'There does seem to be a degree of confusion about what exactly happened.'

'Franz, a urine-soaked indoor pot plant is not confusing. The publican can be trusted. It's his word against a drunken officer. We should be thankful he's not pressing charges.'

'Why would he? The force is his personal goldmine.'

'Be that as it may. It's disgusting, unacceptable behaviour. And be advised that for internal purposes this presents an ideal opportunity for me to implement a transfer. Faye Addison to Launceston. Away from Tredway's bad influence this early in her career.'

'No chance. I fought hard for that position.'

'So you did. But it's quiet in the south.'

'Walter, I'm training her to do tough work. You can't just terminate that because of Rafe.'

'I said, Franz, that this creates an opportunity. I've been looking for an opportunity.'

'Look somewhere else.'

'Are you telling me my job?'

'What's it sound like?'

His lips are pinched. He can't believe how full of shit I am, how prepared I am to keep taking him on.

'I've made the decision, Franz. I'll be advising HR and Launceston. And Tredway shouldn't think this is the end of the matter, either.'

I walk out of his office. In times past, I've slammed his door behind me. Not today. I'm too angry for that.

NOT SO LONG AGO OUR COMMISSIONER GRIF HUNT HAD TO PERSONALLY quash a rumour that he was lobbying to have a new HQ built at the railyard precinct on the waterfront, alongside what had been a proposal for a new hospital. But why would he, with his view? They say it's better than the view from the Premier's office in the Executive Building, because when Hunt's had enough of waterfront he can saunter to the other end of his office and get a faceful of mountain.

But I'm seeing red, now, not views. Hunt rises from his desk as his secretary ushers me in. He's a big, quiet man, not given to facial expressions. I'd rung him. He knows what's up. He gestures me to a chair. Sighs.

'It's tricky, Franz. Staff assignments at that level aren't my call. Walter advised me of his intention. It's his prerogative.'

'He doesn't need to move her. Lonnie doesn't need her. I've invested a lot of specific training in her, and so for that matter has Tredway. It will be profoundly insulting to all three of us if she's transferred.'

He fondles an earlobe, walks to his waterfront window, looks over the trees of the park at the moored yachts, the tourist passenger vessels, the red, blue and white Antarctic research vessel *L'Astrolabe*.

'The change won't necessarily hurt her. She's just a kid.'

'Even if I agree with that, Walter's doing it to get at me by punishing Rafe. He virtually admits as much.'

'Does he?' Hunt turns to look at me. 'One option,' he says, 'is to put Rafe on notice by instructing him to redouble his efforts to mentor Addison.'

Now we're getting somewhere.

'That sounds reasonable, Grif.'

'You know how I like to work. Inclusion not exclusion. Cooperation not mistrust.'

I nod wise agreement. He sounded dangerously like Walter then, but we both know that he's said it out of necessity. He's the man who wears the heavy brass. He can't be seen to favour a mate over a knob.

His phone burrs once. His secretary.

'On your way, Franz, I'm about to chair a forward estimates focus group.' The lightest of smiles. 'Can't wait.'

I'm at the door when he says, 'How was your long service leave?'

'By the end of today I'll know if it was too long or not long enough.'

We share a chuckle, and out I go. Text message on the way down. I read it as I take the broad old polished steps. Hedda. *srvivng? giz a visit if u need 2.* Thoughtful concern for others, eh? She's my lay preacher without the preacher.

Seated at my desk I begin to sort through emails. The phone rings.

'Heineken.'

'Franz? Walter.'

He needn't have identified himself. I didn't mistake him for Moses or Barack Hussein Obama.

'There's another option,' he says, all smooth-toned. 'I thought I'd run it by you, sound you out.'

'Sure.'

'Just as effective. Tredway needs to show more self-discipline, so I'm prepared to say to him, "Look, Rafe, deal with this, deal with this issue, know your place and above all know your responsibility. Rather than show indiscipline, redouble your efforts with Faye." '

'That sounds good, Walter. I'll go with that.'

'Whoa, Franz. There will be procedures.'

'Of course. But nothing has changed.'

That fractional silence. 'In the material sense, no, but I'm obviously happy you agree with the course I'm taking. Seems a good result.'

'I think so. I'll tell Rafe and Faye?'

'No. They don't need to know that we discussed sending her north and decided against it.'

'Okay.'

We disconnect. Liar liar pants on fire. Hunt gave him no option.

I'm barely back in my office when Faye walks in.

'What is it?'

She's thin, fragile, trembling, but she's also defiant. 'Can I just say something?'

'Please.'

'Rafe has been so – he has just helped me so much. He ...'

'What, Faye?'

'He ...'

Her eyes glisten. 'Am I going to Launceston?'

'No.'

'But I thought ...'

'Rafe's a fine detective. We'll look after you. And you'll do Tasmania proud. But there'll be suffering along the way, and you won't necessarily see it coming.'

'You told me that long ago.'

'Long ago? Then perhaps it's close, now.'

I'VE TWO WORK INDULGENCES, ADDICTIONS YOU MIGHT SAY. STRONG black percolated coffee and liquorice allsorts. Don't care about the type of coffee beans, but the allsorts are a different matter. I source mine from a particular retailer in North Hobart, who makes them on the premises with a machine whose patent reads 'Birmingham, England, 1935'. Why does big bad Pufferfish eat kiddie treats? Energy and regularity, that's why. Now, with a mug of the hot black stuff in front of me on my desk, Rafe and Faye seated, she with a file on her lap, I place a small brown bag on the desk, extract an allsort, pop it in my gob, chew slowly. Faye seems fascinated, though she's seen the ritual many times. I rarely offer my allsorts to anyone. Well, to Hedda once, and she screwed up her mouth in distaste at the very idea.

'Okay.' I push my chair back. 'The Collins-Bower case.' I gesture Rafe. 'Maestro, take it from the top.'

'No worries, boss. As if you know absolutely nothing?'

'I wasn't here, remember?'

'Okay. This is the second weekend after you clocked off. Warwick Collins-Bower and his wife Virginia live up at Fern Tree. They migrated here from England, he taught classics at the uni and he retired about ten years ago. She's about his age.'

'They're both seventy-two,' Faye says.

'When he was in England he specialised in Egyptology. He …'

'And what do you know about Egyptology, Rafe?'

'Mate, that it's Egypt with "ology" tacked on! Seriously, I should be boning up on that shit?'

'Faye?'

'Well, the study of ancient Egypt.'

'Course it is,' Rafe says. 'Anyway, Warwick Collins-Bower, who's been in a wheelchair since a car accident way back in England …'

'In 1978 outside Oxford,' Faye says. 'He rolled his car into a ditch. Alcohol may have been involved.'

'You asked our English colleagues for the crash report?'

'Yes.'

'Good.'

'Anyway, he arranged a conference here of the Australasian chapter of the World Society of Egyptologists. And he invited as keynote speaker the bloke Sir Roy Hume, also of Oxford. They had been colleagues there.'

I take a sip of coffee. Very good. Didn't have a drop at the shack.

'For how long?'

'Began when they were both students at Oxford. They got stuck into hieroglyphics and stuff.'

' "And stuff"?'

Rafe shrugs. 'Ancient Egypt …'

'Faye?'

'Well, um, actually they did groundbreaking work on something called the Meroitic script, which I think was used all across that part of Africa. They spoke it in Sudan. This is hundreds of years BC. The script has been deciphered, but not the actual language. What Mr Collins-Bower and Mr Hume did was to look for new letters of the script.'

'That's right,' Rafe says, anxious to be up with her, 'And that's where it went pear-shaped. And this is where Mrs Collins-Bower's best mate comes in. Sally Swanston of Sandy Bay. See, Virginia confided in her. So everything we've got from this point is Sally's word.'

'Would she stack up as a reliable witness?'

'Oh yeah, she'd impress a jury. She'd convince the waverers that Warwick wanted to top Virginia'.

'Mrs Swanston came forward on the same day Mrs Collins-Bower's disappearance was made public,' Faye says.

'Okay. So what's Virginia alleged to have done to deserve getting topped?'

'This goes back to after Warwick's crash. When was it again, Faye?' Rafe grins at her. She shakes her head lightly. Rafe continues, 'After his crash, Warwick and Roy saw less of each other. This made their work become competitive. And how about this, unbeknown to her husband, Virginia had a fling with Roy. Warwick, with more time on his hands as a paraplegic, began to work on some new theories and he reckoned he was about to discover five new letters of the Merro, Mer …'

'Meroitic,' Faye says sweetly.

'Yeah, but Virginia thinks that she inadvertently said something about the letters to Roy, and then guess what, boss?'

'Roy claimed a sensational breakthrough discovery.'

'Yep. Warwick had no way of knowing how, because he didn't know about the affair. He had major suspicions about Roy, but suspicions are no good. Roy became the "Sir" and Warwick and Virginia emigrated to Tassie. End of story, you might think. But no. Apparently, Virginia was consumed with guilt at what she'd thought she'd done, i.e. unwittingly cruelled her husband's lifetime goal.'

Coffee. A second allsort.

'How can we know that Roy Hume didn't independently discover the new letters?'

Rafe looks at Faye. As if to say, well go on then Miss Straight 'A's, your turn. She begins flicking through the file on her lap, the record of interview with Sally Swanston. Finding what she wants she quotes from it. The very words of the vanished Virginia as told to Sally Swanston: ' "Warwick had sole access to a British Museum parchment manuscript that he worked on for years to prove the five new letters. The reason he had sole access to it was because he'd made a photocopy of it, and the original was subsequently destroyed by mishandling when the Museum relocated some holdings. He'd never shown it to Roy and there is no other way the letters could be shown to be part of the Meroitic script".'

'We'll let the experts nut that one out. Alright, Virginia's consumed with guilt. What then?'

'Six months ago', Rafe continues, 'she confessed to Warwick. After he accepted the invitation to plan the conference. This is, y'know, quite a few decades after the deed.'

'She confesses to her husband that she had an affair with his once-best friend and probably also slipped him the vital information?'

'Yeah.'

'Mhm. Brave. Cathartic, I suppose. And?'

'Apparently Warwick slept on it, and next day said all is forgiven. Too long ago to worry about it now. And he also said, not only do I forgive you, but I'll ask Sir Roy to give the keynote. Big-hearted, hey? For a crusty old bloke in a wheelchair, because I tell you boss, he's crusty. Up himself like you wouldn't know. Well, the conference began. Sir Roy gave his address. Warwick, in reply, sharing the stage with him, lets fly. He starts shouting, accusing him of plagiarism. All hell breaks loose. Sir Roy's devastated. So's Virginia. In fact, she spends that night at Sally's place, tells her all. Within twenty-four hours Sir Roy's on a flight home. But, there was that sighting of him with Virginia earlier that day.'

'Where? How credible?'

'Sandy Bay Woolworths roof car park. Young car-washer reckons it was them, getting into a hire car. He remembers because he said the woman – if it was Virginia – seemed upset. And his description of her was good: short, slim, longish grey hair, light as a feather.'

My mobile burrs. Ah, Magnus Salisbury, my old mate. It'll be good to catch up with him. Later.

'Go on.'

'Virginia goes missing. Warwick reports it. He says she came home after staying the night away, said she was going for her daily walk on one of the mountain tracks. As you know, boss, we scoured that bloody mountain. Us, TROGs, SES, chopper, cadaver dog, mountain experts. Unless she's in some humungous crevice, no way she perished up there.'

Mhm. Five letters, eh? And five options, what we call MAMES – Misadventure. Abduction. Murder. Elopement. Suicide.

'How about your interview with Sir Roy in Oxford?'

Rafe shakes his head. 'Nothing doing, boss. He denies ever being in a car with her. Says he only spoke to her once, before the conference started. And totally denied plagiarism.'

'Expensive interview for no result.'

'Tell you what, though! I went to Lords and watched the Poms stitch up the West Indies. Jeez, I had no idea that ground slopes so much.'

'I'm glad the Tasmanian Police Force was able to assist you in making that observation. But your real suspicions are about Warwick?'

'Shit yeah. Bloke's suss.'

'Meaning?'

Faye interrupts, interprets. 'Because he's arrogant he almost invites suspicion.'

'Good, Faye, good, that's intriguing. Is he playing a game with us?'

'He wished us luck with the search warrant,' Rafe says. 'And boss, believe me, we went through his place like Red Kelly's chilli sauce through an Eskimo. We even paid to hold onto and use the cad-dog we'd loaned from the Vics for the mountain search. Even opened one of those big wooden things that they used to stash dead Egyptians in, you know what I mean.'

No I don't. A raised Pufferfish eyebrow cues Faye to again strut her stuff.

'Mr Collins-Bower has a large standing wooden sarcophagus in his house. It's in the shape of the goddess Queen Nefertiti.'

'Where in his house?'

'A kind of museum annexe.'

'Bloke's a nutcase, boss. Why doesn't he just go and live in flippin' Egypt?'

In the near distance an ambulance siren sounds, and I imagine it scattering cars at the Davey Street-Sandy Bay Road intersection.

'So you both rate Warwick Collins-Bower the prime suspect?'

'For sure.'

'Yes.'

'Problem is, not easy from a wheelchair.'

'Could he have hired someone?'

'We've looked at his bank withdrawals. No single big sum, but he has made quite a few withdrawals over the past six months or so that would add up. About twelve ks I think.'

Faye checks her file. 'Twelve thousand five hundred, in withdrawals of either a thousand or five hundred.'

'What did he say about them?'

'Bonuses for his personal carer. He's not short of a dollar, by the way.'

'She back that up? What's her name?'

'Yeah, well, she confirmed he gives her cash now and again. We didn't go into actual specifics.'

'Cristobel da Souza. Each morning she cleans the place and makes his lunch and dinner.'

'He doesn't require hygiene care?'

'No, apparently he can stand, use the loo, use a seat-bath.'

'Okay, thanks for all that. As I'm now I-C this investigation, I'll wander up there and introduce myself.'

'Want us along?'

'No. We don't want him to think we're snooping.'

Their expressions, as they rise, are quizzical. Aren't cops supposed to snoop?

'You'd put him straight on guard and he'd know what to say. Me he has to work out.'

IN MY UNMARKED COMMODORE I EASE OUT OF DAVEY SQUARE'S CAVERNOUS underground car park, cavernous because it also needs to accommodate paddy wagons and ADF personnel carriers, not that Taswegians turn mob at the drop of a hoodie but because, when this place was purpose-designed in the early 1960s, the Cold War was hot, the Vietnam War had taken root and a general sense of paranoia pervaded official thinking. A nasty bruised sky hangs over Hobart. Like a torn sheet, strips of cloud are pouring down the mountain's lined face, promising mayhem. Add a monster king tide, pushing water to dangerously high levels in the waterfront docks, and our little city seems under siege.

Forested Huon Road winds past the Summerleas Road turnoff, way above the city. The Collins-Bowers – she's officially a missing person but just as officially there's still two of them – live at the end of a winding sealed driveway with plenty of acres and, who would have guessed, a pair of hefty stone animals flanking the porch pillars. Hyenas, they'd be, though the particular dynasty escapes me, eh. I wonder if Mr C-B knows that our dear departed thylacine, victim of a parliamentary decision in the 1880s to put a bounty on it, was commonly known as the hyena?

I park behind a white Kia. It would be quiet here when the wind's not roaring through the trees as it is now. Unusual-looking house, large and reasonably modern, but ponderous in a kind of European way, with small windows in its big walls. Apt for a forest setting I suppose. It would take the mother of all fires to destroy it. I use the weatherworn doorknocker, a large brass bird's head. A stylised vulture? I've been reading some Egyptology and I know the importance of these carrion eaters.

A woman wearing a white cleaner's apron opens the door.

'Yes?'

'Cristobel?' I hold out my ID. 'Detective Inspector Franz Heineken. I was hoping to have a word with Mr Collins-Bower.'

'Oh. Is he expecting you?'

'No.'

She thinks about it for a pointless second or two, then steps aside and gestures me in. 'If you wait here, I'll call him.'

'Thanks.'

The room's large and tasteful enough. Bookshelves overflow with ponderous academic tomes, there is a swanky formal lounge-room area, and some gilt-framed oil paintings hark back to the Collins-Bowers' time in the Old Dart. My eye's drawn to what Faye called the museum annexe beyond the lounge-room space. I wander towards its open double doors, beyond which is an eclectic clutter of all things ancient and Egyptian, including what's presumably the centrepiece, the standing wooden sarcophagus. Have to say I'm impressed. With the size of the thing, it's a good two metres tall, the intricate artwork, the golden female face with her arms crossed over her chest and a striped mane of black-and-gold hair. There are ceramic urns and jars and unusual-looking implements in glass cabinets.

'Who are you?'

He's come up silently behind me, in his wheelchair. Cristobel da Souza stands with her arms folded in the doorway from which he must have come, wheeling himself in silence to within spitting distance of me. I look down at him. Hold out my ID. He takes it, inspects it through silver-rimmed spectacles, scowling to read my details. And maybe satisfy himself that the bleak, cold mugshot is the same as the bleak, cold face hanging over him. He hands it back, staring up at me with ill-concealed venom. His thin hair is silvery smooth, his nose beaklike.

'Mr Collins-Bower, I'm now in charge of the investigation into the disappearance of your wife, Virginia.'

'What happened to the others?'

'I've been away. Detective Tredway deputises for me.'

'Well you can tell him from me he's a clumsy bloody sod. He nearly broke that!' He points angrily at the sarcophagus. 'Yes, in his damn haste to open it. What did he expect to find? Idiot! The thing's three thousand years old and priceless! And empty!'

'I've every faith in my officers. And now that I've introduced myself, perhaps you can tell me if you have any new information regarding your wife's disappearance.'

'Of course not. This has all been profoundly distressing.'

'What, in your opinion, has happened to Virginia?'

'I told them. They recorded every bloody word I said.'

'Would you mind telling me?'

Cristobel's coming forward, and I know she's going to say I'm working the poor bugger up and his heart's dicky and his intestines might pop. But he's noticed her and waved her away, and now he emits a sigh and looks down at the tartan blanket over his legs. 'I believe she asked Roy to take her away with him, he refused, and she killed herself.'

'Not necessarily on the mountain?'

'She knows it like the back of her hand. She'd know where to – but yes, there are other ways of doing it. Don't people jump off the Tasman Bridge all the time?'

'I think Mr Collins-Bower should be resting now.'

'Just one more question. Did you anticipate that your action at the conference might have a seriously negative impact on your wife?'

'What do you bloody think?'

'I take that as a yes.'

'*Please* ...' Cristobel puts a hand on his shoulder and glares at me. She's angrily upset. I like that. It suggests she's not complicit in any foul play he might have engineered. I take one of my business cards from my wallet and hand it to her.

'My direct number.'

She drops it in her apron pocket.

'Thanks for your time Mr Collins-Bower. We'll keep in touch.'

By way of answer he wheels about and punts himself off at considerable speed, leaving her to shoo me out into the spit-flecked wind, the door slamming behind me to test those thick walls.

ON THE DRIVE BACK TO TOWN, ALL DOWNHILL AND A FREEWHEELER'S winding delight, I return the call from Magnus Salisbury, my old mate Magnus who left the TPF under a cloud. He's probably my closest friend after Hedda. I put his voice on speaker. We're brief. And old school. Phones are for communicating information, not yakking. He wants to get me over to his place at Taroona to drink some quality reds with a new moneyed neighbour, Bendt. Not just yet for me. Maybe two weekends' time. That's fine by Magnus. Despite all that has happened, he's at peace with himself in the wake of the wars to clear his name. He's got all the time in the world now. He's a happy bloke, and he expresses it every Thursday evening in local pubs, playing alto sax in an over-60s jazz band, the *Swinging Todgers*. He could have been a sour retiree, instead he makes sweet music. Uptight colleagues in the TPF tried to kill off Magnus and his so-called clique of 'Dirty Apple Isle Dicks', a rule-bending close-knit group investigating white-collar crime. They suggested without proof that he tipped off toffs likely to be skewered. And Magnus didn't help his case by overly fraternishing with a hard nut inmate's bereft girlfriend.

3

I'M SHAVING. THE MOBILE BUZZES. NOT THE FIRST TIME I'VE HAD AN early morning call. Usually only has one meaning. A problem. And it's only day two, eh? Towel round waist, paunch that Hedda rubbed, half a face of snow-white lather. View from lounge-room of weatherboard house: the hillside of stilted houses near McRobie's tip.

'Heineken.'

'Radio Room here sir. A member of the public's just phoned and reported a dead body, at Outer North Head past Roaring Beach.'

'Foul play?'

'Definitely. The body's described as in a bag in a shallow grave, on a small beach.'

'Gender?'

'Male.'

'On my way. Contact Tredway and Addison and tell them to get in ASAP.'

CERTAIN PROCEDURAL PRIORITIES KICK IN. FIRST, THE INDIVIDUAL reporting the crime needs to be prevented from doing a runner, in case he or she's associated with the deed. In this case, highly unlikely. A Mr Steve Beecham, a well-known maritime archaeologist who once had a local TV series, made the discovery with a metal detector. He's agreed to stay at the site. Second, the area needs to be cordoned off as a crime scene. In this case, the township of Nubeena's cop is already on his way there. Third, the body, indeed the entire crime scene zone, needs to be left untouched as far as that is possible. Inevitably, forensic evidence gathered at the scene will play a significant role in solving the case.

We conferred briefly at HQ, I made a few calls, glanced at the dodgy weather, shrugged into my trusty shit-brown overcoat, and now we're in two cars giving the Tasman Highway a right workout, silent blue and red lights doing their thing. Forensics won't be far behind, with a small team of uniforms to do as told in the matter of transferring the body into a TPF custom-built refrigerated corpse cart, as we charmingly call those vehicles.

Rafe and Faye are behind me. No chance I'd let him lead, that would be an invitation to him to try to crack 140 ks. Along this narrow and winding two-laner, all the way from Hobart to Dunalley, then threading south through the Forestier Peninsula to the Tasman Peninsula at Eaglehawk Neck, and looping back west to Nubeena and Roaring Beach, then along a rutted strip to the isolated beach at Outer North Head. On this small beach deep water crashes onto steep sand, so that only under specific conditions of tide and wind is the area surfable. Dumpers rule. And I know from experience that you're better off fishing from a boat fifty metres out. From the shore, your tackle just gets mauled by the severe undertow. Meaning? Few use the area. Fewer still know that it exists. Meaning? Whoever stashed the victim there felt secure in doing so.

The mild, post-storm sunshine of this particular morning is trending rapidly back to chill and gloom as I step from the Commodore at the end of the track. Rafe skids to a dusty halt beside me. Nearby is Sergeant Woods of Nubeena's TPF Falcon and the marine archaeologist's old Beemer. The two men are nowhere to be seen. We take the path into scrub, bashed just wide enough to allow surfers' and bushwalkers' passage and, now, carriage of a corpse. Unless, of course, the deed was carried out on the beach.

Two minutes' walk, tiny scrub wrens darting about in front of us, and we're suddenly looking at a gob-smacking view of vast Storm Bay, much of south-eastern Tasmania's fractious coastline, and the direct route to Antarctica. Woods and Beecham – just by the man's posture you can see he's taken a hit – cut a strange sight standing together a good way from the large rectangle of blue and white crime scene tape hanging limply off a pile of stakes, right up at the back of the steep beach. Woods was probably going to use those stakes for his tomatoes, assuming he's obeyed the Tasmanian rule to never plant them before Show Day.

Woods, gesturing Beecham to wait, hurries forward. He wants to get in a word, so I stop, wait.

'Franz, glad you're here.'

'How are you, Woodsy? Rafe you know, and this is Detective Constable Faye Addison.'

'It's not a good sight, Franz, and Steve's not a well man.'

'Sure. I believe the corpse has been there some time.'

'My word yes –'

'So we can rule out the perps being in the vicinity?'

'Long gone.'

'Cause of death, Woodsy?'

'Head wound. Oh, good luck, mate. Hold your nose …'

On we go.

'Very sorry about this, Mr Beecham. How did you discover the body?'

'Only because of the king tide. That's why I was here. The *Goede Fortuun* was wrecked somewhere here in 1648, and I'm convinced she smashed straight into this beach, or what would have been a much narrower beach then, and, and …'

The enormity of it all plagues him once again.

'Thanks, Mr Beecham. Sergeant Woods will take some notes from you, if you're okay with that now. Perhaps go to the cars.'

He nods.

'Rafe, Faye, come.'

We step onto the beach of soft, damp sand with its invisible gremlins slurring and harrying our footsteps. As we approach Woods's demarcation site, airborne slicks of putrefying human flesh become waves of throaty nausea. Rafe and I know what's ahead. Welcome to major crime, Faye.

Rafe says to Faye, and he says it as casually as he can, 'Mate, tip. When you look down at him, clamp your teeth together real tight.' She nods. 'Because there's nothing Forensics likes worse than last night's stir-fry on a ripe corpse.'

'I can handle myself.'

'He couldn't!'

Rafe gags. Must have gulped in a dose of death trying to laugh at it.

THE HIGH TIDE'S HAMMERED THE BEACH, SUCKING GREAT QUANTITIES of sand away and depositing all manner of vegetative debris on the tide-line, large bull kelp anchors included. The grave, probably dug to a depth of about a metre, would have been all but exposed by the time Beecham ran over it with his metal detector. What we see is the top portion of a large grey cotton-canvas bag, part of an image printed on it dully visible. The tines of a stag's antlers. A deer bag, its drawstring loosely closed. I kneel, pull apart the drawstring, lift the canvas.

26

'My old man used to have one of them,' Rafe says, matter of factly, 'to take the venison home.'

The corpse is face down. First impressions at such times are always a jumble of surreal intensity. The back of the head, blood-blackened and misshapen, took a violent blow, or a number of blows. The shoulders and arms in the brightly patterned T-shirt are so swollen they seem about to burst. But neither maggots nor sand weevils got to him. The drawstring must have been mighty tight. Lacking the maggot life cycle might make estimating time of death more difficult, though he's been dead a good while. A skinhead. And some kind of thin chain around the neck, a personal adornment.

I stand. Gesture. Rafe, then Faye, kneel and scrutinise.

Then we back off a bit, turn seawards for the mild onshore breeze.

'Clubbed with something blunt, hard,' Rafe says, 'the way the wound is right across the base of the skull.'

'Why in a game-hunting bag?' Faye asks.

'Transport,' I suggest. 'And they've made two mistakes already. Not everyone owns a deer bag. And the body's well preserved. William will be pleased.'

I'm referring to Dr William Doll, our dapper long-time head of the Forensic Unit. He'll be in his element. No dirt and, hopefully, no DNA-destroying agents like petrol or alcohol. Even rain washes vital evidence away. So it's a reasonable start. Not bad as murders go.

BEECHAM, OLD STAGER THAT HE IS, JUST HAPPENS TO HAVE A COMFORTING flask of tea in his car, in which he and Woods are sitting while he makes his statement. In the time before the arrival of Forensics and the uniforms, the three of us have divvied up and scoured the area, looking for whatever might be of value. Cigarette butt, beer can, chewing gum wrapper, blunt instrument, knife, cartridge shell, name and address of killer, anything. Given the weather and the fact that the burial took place a week or more ago, we've got, as they say, Buckleys. No matter. It's procedure. And a breakthrough can turn on the most unlikely evidence.

I'm slowly walking the bush path when I hear vehicles arrive. Instructions float through the scrub. I walk out to meet them. Doll, half a dozen uniforms, and a photographer are putting on their orange and lime green forensic overalls, masks and gloves.

'Morning, Franz!'

'Hello, William. We have a body in ex. cond. for you.'

'Good-o.' He glances about. 'I've often wondered what it's like here.'

I know what he means. William's a mad keen yachtie, with a nice Sailmaster B45 he sails from Lindisfarne, and he would have tacked his way through these waters any number of times on the way to the Dunalley Canal and Blackman Bay, the short cut to the east coast.

'Male, about fifty from what I can see of the face. Nice and snug in a deer bag.'

Doll raises his eyebrows. 'Unusual. Should help you.'

'We're hoping.'

On the beach I watch Doll taking it all in, the distant battered and bruised low landforms, the immensity of unhappy sky above them, the wreckage of flotsam scattered along the tideline, and the sand all churned up as if nature tried to get at the grave.

'No weather for a burial,' Doll murmers, as his first observation.

I just nod. And have an infant thought. If they can make a mistake like this, they can make another.

Once Doll's carried out his initial examination and made some remarks into his recorder, the photographer gets busy. We watch. Then, after the forensic examination, uniforms get to work, carefully shovelling a moat around the grave, until the entire bag is exposed. It's big, probably 90 by 200 centimetres, the material strong and durable, although by the faded look of the image, a large fallow stag with an impressive set of antlers, this bag's pretty old. Four pairs of tough gloved hands carefully lift the bag by its corners, taking care not to allow it and its occupant to sag in the middle, and they just as carefully place it on a stretcher. We watch them walk away with it, disappear onto the narrow path. I look into the grave. Nothing in it. Not that I expected a calling card. Still, I get Rafe to poke around with a spade. Even smart crims do dumb things from time to time.

THE FORENSIC UNIT IS AT THE HOSPITAL, FOR ACCESS TO ITS BIOLOGICAL and chemical services. I front up with Rafe and Faye for the prelim results of Doll's examination. We're in the Forensics room, adjacent the hospital morgue. The body's now face up, naked, on a sterilised white plastic sheet on an examination trolley. Neatly clipped to a whiteboard is a large, high res. coloured photographic print of the wound to the back of the head. Clipped alongside it is an X-ray of the skull. In a small tray on a small table is the chain that was around the corpse's neck. It has a basic key ring on which are two keys. The clothes – T-shirt, jeans, socks, fancy pointed shoes – are laid out on the floor next to the deer bag.

In death the face is neither serene nor anything else, just dead and discoloured and losing shape. The nose is recently broken. And there's a distinct mark on the temple between the left ear and left eye.

'What's the hole, William?'

'The exit point of a high velocity bullet. It went in here, shot from close range.' He points to a smudge on the photograph near the base of the skull, then at the X-ray. 'In through the lamboidal suture, rupturing the spinal nerve at the C2 vertebra and chipping the mandibular bone on its way out.'

'That doesn't explain the bashing to the back of the head.'

'No, and you're going to have to come up with some ideas. He was hit at the base of the skull with great force, by an object that significantly haemorrhaged the local area. There are lots of tiny grains deep in the tissue and also in the blood clots. Analysis will probably show them to be cement or brick particles. But he didn't fall from a height. This was a single, powerful blow from behind – just as the bullet came from behind.'

'Running away.'

'You would think so, Franz. The trajectory of the bullet is slightly upward, which is uncommon.'

'From what distance was the blow delivered?'

'We'll make reasonably accurate suppositions about that. A stand and deliver impact breaks skin, tissue and bone in a way that a delivered missile does not.'

'So the blow could have been to disable him, or stop him, the bullet to finish him off.'

'Entirely possible.'

'And what about these marks on the skin, William? Steps?'

'Oh yes.' He traces a forefinger just above a thick bruised line across the chest, another across the midriff, others across the legs. 'He fell hard down a flight of short steps. Carpeted, or else the lines would be finer and would probably have broken the skin, even though he's not that heavy. The fall probably smashed his nose. And you see, there are no such lines across the palms of his hands, which you would expect to instinctively break your fall.'

'So he could have been unconscious, or even dead, when he fell?'

'Possibly. I'm more inclined to consider that he was running away from his assailant, who threw something at him, causing him instant concussion, so that he fell down the stairs like a sack of potatoes. There he lay, bleeding from both the nose and the back of the head. He was then shot in the back of the head. I suggest, gentlemen, that you look for a location testing this theory.'

'Any idea of the kind of gun, bullet?' Rafe asks. He knows plenty about firearms.

'The cleanness of the bullet's passage made me think of the deer bag,' Doll replies.

'Yeah, my thoughts exactly,' Rafe says. 'A combination of shooter and shell that drops the animal fast but does minimal damage to the meat.'

The moment enables us to pause and contemplate in silence. Where, when, why.

'Microscopic analysis may reveal more,' Doll eventually says. 'Ditto the stains on the victim's clothes. Blood, obviously, but there may be something else. And at this stage I estimate death was up to ten days ago.'

'I read in one of the trainee manuals,' Faye says, 'that a sign of some ex-crims is keys around the neck, so they don't have to carry a wallet and stuff and be identified that way.'

'Could be. That one's a car key. What the hell's the other?' I pick it up, examine it. A good 7 centimetres long, its dulled alloy and slight bentness suggest a well-used, rare old door key. I remove the two keys from the chain, hand them to Faye. 'All yours. Make sure you have dupes made.'

Doll hands her an FU evidence bag. She seals the keys in it. Doll records the handover in his computer. I find myself again looking at the face, the shorn head, the pointy features made more so as the moisture-deprived skin tightens.

'William, one thing ...'

'Yes, Franz?'

'Is it my imagination, or are there two tones to the skin? The forehead and cheek skin are darker than the chin and lips, and even round here, the upper shoulders are paler than the rest of the back.'

'I saw that, yes, and recorded it as,' – he goes back his computer – ' "noticeable discolouration after death". Why?'

'What if he had a head of long hair, a beard and moustache, and they were shaved shortly before he died?'

Doll peers down at the torso, eyeballing the gradations of grey, which on a corpse like this, with its savage wound, don't stand out.

'Franz, it's possible. Particularly if he had a tan.'

'Makes him a blow-in, then,' Rafe says. 'Some dodgy character from the big island, Queensland, maybe. Fits with the loud T-shirt, too.'

'And those are crocodile skin shoes', Faye says.

A frisson of excitement steals through the room. We don't have much, but neither do we have nothing. Keys. A deer bag. A possible change of appearance. At this early stage, we'll take them all.

4

HUNT REQUIRES A PERSONAL BRIEFING. HE'S CONSTANTLY TALKING TO his Minister and to other senior pollies as well, and at the breaking of a sensational murder he needs to be absolutely across all the known facts. Walter then calls a press conference, at which an identikit of the victim, standing and fully clothed, is released. To do the job properly, our artist had to have the corpse's eyelids propped open. Pale blue-green eyes with copper flecks, slightly slanted, slightly sunken in the sockets. Shifty, even in the afterlife. This evening, the image will appear in the electronic media from one end of the Australian continent to another, and tomorrow the newspapers will go to town on him, saturation in Tassie, prominent elsewhere, because news editors know the civic importance of these things. They also have to sell their product, and the public loves a good, safe shiver. It'll be a major shock, too, for those responsible, and that might trigger another mistake. Leaving him in the deer bag wasn't smart. Whereas our smart idea is to leave small but crucial pieces of information out of our media release. We're saying that the victim was shot in the head at close range, but not exactly where in the head. If the media wants that detail, we'll fudge it. We pigs are sneaky bastards. And no mention of keys.

Faye's got her keys. They'll be a good test for her. And Rafe and I will be driving north shortly to start our investigations into all things deer. We'll need to manage it with care. Deer hunting is popular in Tassie. Deer farming's respectable. Yet already emails and phone calls are coming in linking the 'barbaric sport' of stag trophy hunting with shady characters. At times like this it's more important than ever that a cop be seen to be neutral. Myself, I've no worry about that – I never discriminate in the matter of who I'm unpleasant to.

I stick my head around their door. No Faye. Rafe's working his phone setting up interviews. He looks quizzically at me. I use two fingers to indicate that I'm going walkabout. He nods. I then use the same two fingers to indicate scissors cutting hair. Again he nods. Who said he was thick?

HOBART'S POPULATION IS GENERALLY CONSIDERED TO BE 150,000, ABOUT the same as an average Melbourne suburb, or three decent MCG footy crowds. So the CBD's tiny, like a toy city. You could almost imagine a child's chubby fingers moving things around. Yet we're a miniature of everything Oz. Macchiato, McDonalds, KFC, Harvey Norman, RM Williams, RSL, Your ABC. And traditional men's barber shops. One of which, in Elizabeth Street, in the action as it has been since the 1950s, is well known to me. It has the red and white pole outside, the shiny black-and-white tiled floor, two classy old green leather and chrome elevator chairs in which the business is done, nice big gilt mirrors, bottles of hair products. Once upon a time I regularly sat in one or other of those chairs, until Hedda broke the habit by giving me a shaver, suggesting I start self-administering a number 2 or 3 to flatter the bald spot and enter the twenty-first century, albeit a good many years late.

A cowbell sounds as I enter, a loud, unequivocal noise. The man I want, Knacker McConachie, all 155 centimetres of him, is reclining in his white barber's coat in one of his chairs, most of the way through a fat paperback novel. He glances over a diminutive shoulder, sees it's me, swings around in the chair. Its momentum pops him out of it like a seed.

'Mr Heineken! Long see no time. How are ya?'

'Good thanks, Knacker. What's the book?'

He shows me its cover. I shake my head.

'Ending's crap. Real letdown. How's business?'

'Hair grows. So what can I do you for, Detective Sherlock Marlowe?'

I stand my briefcase on his magazine table and take from it three enlarged high resolution photographs of the face of the dead man. I put them down on the table, like big kid cards alongside one another.

'Oh yeah, him, hey', Knacker says. 'Poor bastard. Hey, what's worse than a hard-on at the beach? A stiff in the sand!' He brays with laughter. For such a small bloke he's got a majestic set of long, crooked yellow teeth with gaps, like a jockey who nicked his nag's dentures.

'I'm rolling on the floor, Knacker. The thing is, look at those skin colours. Look at that head shave. I reckon he had it done not long before he died.'

'Maybe.'

'Do the up-market salons do skinhead jobs like that?'

'Do rhinoceroses lay eggs, Captain Fancypants?'

'So one of your merry band of traditional Taswegian haircroppers may have had this bloke in his chair.'

'True enough. But he'd have recognised the sorry bastard on the tv, don't ya reckon?'

'Funnily enough I did think of that. But you know how the business works.'

'Leave no turn unstoned, Mr Heineken.'

'Ask around Knacker, if you wouldn't mind. You've got my number.'

'I will, but don't count your breath, Kojak.'

'Nor will I hold my chickens. Ask around.'

WALTER, BLESS HIM AND HIS WONDERFUL FAMILY, WANTS CHAPTER and verse on how I plan to proceed, so that he can relay it upstairs and run it by the TPF media secretariat. I suspect he may also remind me to drill down on every scrap of evidence. So I invite him to drill himself down and join us. Just making sure I'm in Rafe and Faye's office when he arrives. Why? Because I'd like him to reflect upon the fact that their shared space has a unique part-messy, part-neat chemistry about it, an atmosphere of intimately shared cop oxygen and broader youthful energy, which he wished to destroy.

When the great man strides in, having first peered expectantly through Heineken's beckoningly open door, Rafe and Faye are seated at their desks, and I'm elbows down at their communal table. This table is their in-tray, out-tray, today's *Mercury*, yesterday's sandwich crusts (Rafe's). I'm poring over a 1:500 000 Land Map of Tasmania that demarcates the no less than 13 types of ownership-cum-management on this island. Popular perception is that Tasmania is a small island. World geography defines Tasmania as a large island. Look and learn.

'Morning, team.' Walter rubs his palms together. 'Let's get cracking.' He advances into the room exuding brittle camaraderie. He searches for a cool spot to park his pinstriped carcase. Unfortunately, the only coolness in here is radiating off self and self's offsiders, directed at him. Walter leans against the table, nods.

'Narrow the focus, Franz. Like it.'

'Yes. The poaching box.'

I feel him look surprised, as if this is no time to discuss the cooking of eggs, but like an amateur on ice skates who ought to know how it's done, he recovers his balance quickly, watches with interest as I tap out a ragged rectangle on the map. Derwent Bridge, Pontville, St Helens, Launceston.

'Logically, we start in here. It's where the deer are, farmed and wild, and the hunters, legal and illegal.'

'Who are you going to talk to?'

'Rafe's drawn up a list. Farmers, lodge operators, and a few individuals of interest.'

'Have to be a hunter,' Walter muses. 'Who else'd own a huge deer bag?'

'Cullers, for one,' Rafe advises him. 'Registered, unregistered.'

'And what about the keys, Faye?'

'A Mitsubishi van, I'll know the year and model soon. Not sure yet about the other, it's old …'

Walter nods. 'Okay. Let's get the model and have an image sent to the media ASAP, but through me, please Faye.'

'I think you should put some spin on it.'

Walter frowns at my suggestion. He's a stickler for doing things properly. Spin is only permissible when he's the first to have thought of it. I watch his lips tighten. Surely the man's not going to have a hissy fit.

'Spin? Why?'

'Because the perps don't know about the keys. Let's have them thinking we know more than we do.'

'I'll consider it, Franz. Call in before COB if you would.'

'Sure.'

'Luck all.' He strides out. I'm as unmoved as I was when he entered, looking down at the map. My worry is the age of the bag. William Doll said the DNA of its many stains may be too degraded to positively identify. Still, they'll tell some kind of story. And as Rafe and I have already agreed, not only deer hunters use deer bags. I move away from the map and take a look at the printed images scattered across Faye's desk. Keys. Lots of old keys.

'Progress?'

'Not much. No local locksmith's got it registered. Too old.'

'For all we know it opens the dunny door at Waldheim Lodge,' Rafe says helpfully.

'How old is old, Faye?'

'They think the 1930s.'

'Mhm … Well, if he's a blow-in, maybe he was staying in an old hotel. Too much of a bogan to use a tarted-up B&B.'

'Hotel, boss?' Rafe's sceptical. 'There'd be a room number. I reckon it's the door to an old cottage or something. Out in the bush. He's a poacher, after all, well, maybe. So he's got a place somewhere out there.'

'Except that no one recognises him. Keep at it, Faye. You never know.'

RAFE AND I ARE HEADING NORTH. DEER BUSINESS. MY CAR, HE DRIVING, me content to be chauffeured. We've obediently chuntered along the traffic-heavy, unattractive Brooker Highway, the multi-lane bitumen river barging its way between homes, light industries, service outlets, playing fields, the Royal Showgrounds, Elwick Racecourse, the great and shocking dome of the Derwent Entertainment Centre – alien spaceships welcome, free park first hour – until opening out a bit along the river and an increased speed limit, Rafe's invitation to gun her. He'll have checked if there are any radars on our route, advised them of our urgent business. Yes, it's urgent, but shaving ten minutes off the journey won't help us much. Try telling that to Det. Tredway, not that I care. As long as he doesn't kill me, he's welcome to go as fast as the Commodore reasonably allows.

We enter the Valley of Love in quick time. Rolling hills, river bends, black swans, banks of reed.

'What if he *is* a poacher?' Ralph muses.

Hobart's city slickers use the Love term derogatively, as if the good folk of the Derwent Valley are all rough, tough, chain-smoking hillbillies. It's an ancient enmity, in which the convicts of Hobarton looked down their noses at the convicts of New Norfolk. Today, it ensures fierce rivalry on the footy fields.

'What if he is?'

Rafe's fishing. So am I. We've not much else to go on, and it's nagging away.

'Scenario, boss. He double-crosses or otherwise mightily pisses off his fellow poacher, or maybe his boss. He's gone one step too far, he's become a liability, maybe he knows something he shouldn't. So, bang, goodbye.'

'That means premeditated.'

'Could be … Maybe they smacked him on the back of the head while he was asleep.'

'Then shot him?'

'That's what I'm thinking.'

'I like Doll's theory. I think we have to assume he was running away and the blow was meant to stop him.'

'Okay, still could be premeditated. The intent was to kill him. Just that they needed more than a bullet. Y'know, they lured him somewhere and once there he tried to do a runner.'

'That's got possibilities.'

We hum past the paper mill, its bright white steam clouds hanging over the tranquil river. Tethered goats, old car bodies.

'Yeah. He's called to account for something wrong. "Why'd you sell the venison and antler velvet to a rival, you dead bastard!" '

'Rafe, not even rogue shooters murder for a bit of bloody meat, even if it does cost more than wagyu beef.'

'So something else then. They ship dope as well as venison to mainland markets.'

'Then it's no longer really about poaching.'

He sighs. He tried. But he's not giving it away. Nor would I want him to. I want him to keep thinking, talking.

'Tell you what, boss. When my old man used to take me hunting I met some pretty ordinary fellas.'

'You said so. Which is why I want you talking the talk to Pennington.'

Charlie Pennington is one of our calls today. He owns a hunting lodge well into the hills beyond Bothwell.

' "Ordinary", how?'

Rafe thinks about it, weighs his response. 'A fair few of these boys are in cammo and seriously gunned up. It's nothing for them to stalk a stag most of a day, commando crawling a chunk of that. You have to see the dedication to believe it, and they'll do anything for one other. For some, it's all about the toughest of tough bloke culture. Hard-edged. And, you don't cross one of your own who'd thought he was your mate. Specially if he's got a Ruger K77 Frontier or something in his paw when he works out what a scumbag you are.'

'Mhm … That was back then. Getting on for twenty years ago, right?'

'Let's see. My old man took me hunting every season from when I was about ten until they divorced, so that would've made me sixteen. Year I left school anyway. Dad turned me into a shooter, which is why I joined the force. He wouldn't have realised that all those days and nights in the bush and in the swag were priming me for my career. It made Mum filthy, not being a gun person, but I reckon I told you all of that.'

'You did.'

'Funnily enough Dad had actually been a mad keen fisho. Bit like you, hey?'

'Keen, not mad.'

'Dunno about that, boss. Anyway, Dad went off to a game lodge in the Shaky Isles one time with some mates, but the rainbows were on strike so they went hunting for red stags instead, and he was hooked from the off. I used to say later on, "Mate, when you start shooting trout we'll know the dementia's set in".' He glances at me. 'You never wanted to shoot?'

I shake my head. 'Sitting in a runabout under a hat with a cold beer suits me. Even if they aren't biting. So what's the attraction of going on a hunt?'

We've eased through New Norfolk, a largish town comfortable on its river banks. We take the bridge over the river and leave the town behind. And stop while a large herd of Friesians ambles across the road from one paddock to another, not five metres in front of the bonnet. The sweet-sharp smell of their turds steaming on the tarmac enters the vehicle, or am I just imagining it?

'As a thrill for a nipper, dropping a spiky takes some beating,' Rafe says. 'The men are all over you with congratulations and, y'know, you've taken possession of this … *thing* – a huge, warm, wild-smelling wild animal. Getting to pose for snaps with your kill is probably the high moment. You took hours to find the bugger, constantly glassing the ridges of the hills and the gullies, sneaking through the bush, maybe it's raining, keep the wind in your face, what a bugger if it turns about, because the deer are off straight away and you gotta start all over again. Boss, I shot my first fallow deer at 150 metres. Resting the Sauer Classic on a tree stump, crosshairs on the middle of the chest, bang, down like a sack of kennebecs.'

The last cow crosses. Rafe accelerates. 'I'd say the feeling is like when you finally lift a trophy after a really tough game of finals footy. You're an exhilarated, buggered hero.'

'That would be why it's called trophy hunting.'

'Yeah, the real purpose. Not meat. It's all about putting a big testosterone-fuelled stag with impressive head gear on your wall.'

'And the mateship.'

'Yeah, that too. Until the mateship goes pear-shaped and the deer bag finds another use.' He laughs. 'Back to square one, boss. Just don't get me started on caping.'

'Were you good at it?'

'No!' He laughs again. 'Too impatient. It's finicky ... Jeez, I could do with a Coke. Why don't they have KFC in the bush? Gotta shoot your own bloody chicken buckets out here!'

'Tell me about caping.'

'Why?'

'Pennington and I didn't always get on well when he was a TROG. I don't want him thinking I'm feeling in the dark, not knowing the territory.'

'Yeah, right, okay.'

Rafe slips me a sideways glance. I don't blame him. He knows something – only something – of the long complexity of my time as a Tasmanian cop. So for him to hear that I may have crossed swords with Charlie Pennington, once a highly regarded senior member of the Tactical Response Operations Group, is news. The kind of news taken in without comment in an unmarked Holden Commodore buffeting along a narrow, empty Apple Isle back road at 120 kph.

Not quite empty. Ahead, and closing fast, a gang of pitch-black forest ravens hop around a bloated wallaby carcase, right in the middle of the road. No devils did the initial work, sadly, which means more meat for the ravens and European wasps. Rafe imperceptibly adjusts the steering. We miss the wallaby – just – and yet even out here the ravens with their sharp silver button eyes are smart enough to miss Rafe – just.

'Boss, the initial cuts around and up the back of the neck are easy enough. But the hardest is to free the ears by cutting below them close to the bone. That's where caping pliers come in, the ear pliers – tell ya, pulling ears inside out is difficult, because the back ear skin needs to be separated from the cartilage at the front of the ear, with a knife tip if you're good enough. Then you mosey your index finger between the eyeball and the bone at the back corner of the eye, and use the knife to separate the inner skin from the bone wall. You need extra sharpness for cutting around the eyes and the preorbitals. Then you probably want a blunt-tip blade for splitting the lip skin without cutting through the lips. The inside lip skin needs to be separated from the outer lip skin. You cut around the gum line inside the mouth. Then you cut through the nose cartilage and it's done. Now you can pull the whole skin intact off the head and Bob's your uncle.'

THE APPROACH ROAD TO CHARLIE PENNINGTON'S LODGE IS SMOOTH, dusty, narrow. His acreage, and there's plenty of it, is near Lake Crescent. Off the beaten track? Absolutely. Pennington Lodge caters to cashed up international clients who want pesticide-free dirt under their fingernails and a night sky untinged by human light, with just the faintest possibility of being woken by the hoarse yip of a thylacine.

Pennington's a bit more thickset these days – like me, eh? – but the no-nonsense military moustache is in place and the baby-blue eyes still twinkle with deceptive mildness.

'How are you, Franz? Good to see you again.'

'And you, Charlie.' I gesture the deer paddocks around their conical hills, the valleys and tiers, stands of increasingly dense trees rising to the far horizons. 'Biggest hobby farm I've seen.'

He laughs.

'My colleague, Detective Rafe Tredway. He joined a couple of years after you cut and run.'

'Best move I ever made. G'day, Rafe, pleased to meet you.'

'And you Charlie. Mate, I'm envious.' They shake firm hands.

We wouldn't be the first to lavish praise on his set-up – the homestead alone has a seriously rustic charm – but he seems to like hearing it from cops at work.

'Let's go to the Lodge, boys.'

We crunch off the driveway gravel onto a well-kept lawn, towards a man-made lake, at the edge of which is the horizontal-timbered Lodge with twin peaked roof and raised verandah all around. Charlie's talking about his clients and the picture's clear. After the day's hard yakka they surely sit on that verandah sipping something cold and golden, watching, through a nectarine sunset, black ducks, grebes and herons, fish breathing. Unless it's cold, in which case open fireplaces are stacked and ready inside.

Charlie steers us through an elegantly quiet foyer, prominent on a wall of which is a Quality Deer Management charter, into the Trophy Room where coffee's waiting. A big, long room with a large picture window fronting the lake. Tas oak floors shine among leather settees and armchairs. Immaculately stocked gun racks line an entire wall. Gleaming knives lie in a glass presentation case, a Bowie classic, a pig sticker, a curved skinner, a drop point. They stand alongside a case of trout flies, dozens of examples of painstaking craftsmanship. On the walls are high-mounted trophies, handsome fallow deer stags with proud sets of antlers, their glass-eyed expressions peculiarly lifelike.

'Wow. I'm a kid in a sweet shop.' Rafe handles one rifle, then another and another, feeling the weight, looking through their scopes out at the lake. I watch Charlie watching him carefully until he recognises the easy weapon handling of a fellow guns 'n' ammo tragic.

He does the coffees, we sit.

'Thanks for your time, Charlie, appreciated. It all begins with this.' I take a colour photo of the deer bag from my jacket pocket, hand it to him. He studies it, nodding.

'Yeah, saw it in the media, ancient old thing.' He puts the photo on the low glass-topped table around which we're sitting.

'Our problem is that we've got bugger all, apart from that bag and the fact that the victim was shot with a soft point, probably a 130, which I believe is standard for fallow deer. There was no ID on the victim and nothing to lead us anywhere, not at this stage anyway. So, Charlie, I've got a fairly straightforward request.' He nods. 'To get from you any information, anything at all, about any individuals known to you who may be capable of this, or who we might usefully talk to.'

'Right. Thought that'd be the ask when you rang me. Still, bit confronting to hear it.' He sits back and folds his arms. 'Asking a bloke to name names.'

'Sure. Understandable.'

My turn to wait. Charlie looks at Rafe, then back at me.

'You know, Franz, I'm big on QDM. It's the future of Tassie's farmed and wild deer herds. I farm five hundred head and my land supports a wild population twice that number. But there are lots of poachers out there. Some just for the pot, almost feel sorry for them, poor white trash as my American clients would say. Others, I'd like to strangle with my bare hands. The pros. They take large stags out of season, they wipe out any number of two-year-olds because their meat is the best, and they'll hunt for antler and leave the wasted corpses just so that Koreans can take their velvet pills and stay horny all night long. It is a real, ongoing problem. But do I know who those professional poachers are? No, because if I did they'd be behind bars now.'

I nod my head slowly, allowing his head of steam to subside. I can see where this is going.

'We obviously consider that professional poachers are likely candidates. But I have to be open-minded at this stage. The disposal of the body suggests panic, rather than seasoned crims at work.'

'So you're asking me do I know any otherwise legit hunters who could do this? Some flaky bastard?'

Again I nod.

'What about shooters who don't do deer?' he asks, buying thinking time. And just thinking, like a good ex-cop.

'Yes, equally possible, whether registered or not.'

In one of those moments that afflict awkward conversations, the three of us simultaneously lean forward and drink coffee.

'Nice brew,' Rafe says, well aware of his rank in this conversation, this early in the piece.

'Yes, I know some flaky characters, Franz. I even know a prominent landowner who probably murdered and weighted his son and dropped him into the middle of Lake Sorell not ten years ago. But naming names … How discreet would you be?'

'Only as much as it takes, Charlie. You know how we operate. I'm a public servant. But yes, I have discretion.'

'Why are Parks and Wildlife so bloody useless when it comes to poachers?'

'Understaffed.'

'Mate, come on, that's not good enough, they're a disgrace.'

'I'm sure they try. Would you like me to put in a word?'

'How about a great big word, Franz? How about a dedicated poaching unit? Isn't that a reasonable price?'

'I'll do what I can.'

'Ta. Well then, I've got some suggestions. Some names.'

I glance at Rafe.

Like a big hound about to be released on the hunt, he whips out his notebook and pen, says eagerly, 'Go for it, Charlie. Shoot.'

5

THE MYSTERY DEEPENS, SEEMING TO INSIST THERE IS NO SOLUTION.
Why has no one recognised the identikit? Not in Tassie, not interstate,
not through Interpol? Because he changed, that's why, I'm convinced of
that. Who changed him?

And there's no CrimTrac match on his prints or DNA.

William Doll's forensic results make interesting reading, like reading
junk mail is interesting, all colour and promise, minimal substance. Four
carpet-type fibres in the matted blood at the base of the neck. Degraded
blood and other bodily fluids impregnated in the deer bag impossible
to identify, probably belonging to both marsupial and mammal species.
Maybe deer, maybe dog, certainly the victim, possibly avian as well.
Some idiots take out raptors as perceived menaces to farm stock. Then
again, shooting road signs is a popular Tasmanian pastime. The fancy
crocodile shoes sell in selected retail outlets in the Northern Territory,
South Australia and New South Wales. His last meal was a lamb kofta,
identifiable because the stomach processes shut down soon after ingestion
of the meal.

But there are two bits of intrigue. First, on one crocodile shoe, and
on the jeans, there are samples of fresh human blood that do not belong
to the victim. Second, the victim once had tattoos below each of the
knuckles of the fists. Either so amateurishly applied that they faded
beyond recognition, or were otherwise scrubbed away long ago in an
effort to destroy them as identifiers. They're letters or numbers, Doll's
not sure.

I NEVER WAS A CANTEEN JUNKIE, GOSSIP AND SLOP DON'T AGREE
with me, but an occasional plate of fish and chips I can handle, plus
it's pissing down, so I'm solo at a table for two, shovelling in blue

grenadier and Table Cape kennebecs when Hedda joins the queue with her Faye equivalent, a drug squad rookie named Troy Seedge. Perhaps his parents had a sense of humour, though I doubt it, because Troy himself, as offspring material, apparently isn't the brightest bead in the doily. But there's plenty of mongrel in him. He's a third dan something-or-other, one up from DS Andover, and he's earned a bit of a name for himself as a fine member of the TROGs. They're not a permanent outfit. Our force is too small for that and they're rarely required in more than twos or threes, and usually then for domestics. The idea was that a weapons and combat expert would be a good fit for the drug branch, so he was moved across from general duties a few months ago. Hedda doesn't mind him. Dog-faithful, was one of her descriptions.

And now she's coming this way with Troy in tow. He's noticeably shorter than her, not least because she's pretty damn tall, and he walks with that squat ambulatory motion induced by pent-up muscles. That and the grim, eyebrowed expression of a young man in a serious world make him vaguely comic. Especially if you're an old cynic like me.

'Mate, how's things?'

'Good thanks Hedda, you? Hello Troy.'

'G'day Mr Heineken.'

Hedda sits. Troy looks around, finds a seat at a nearby table. Hedda's got a side plate of crackers, a wedge of good King Island vintage cheese, via a deal with the chef, because she refuses to touch their processed stuff, a small bunch of grapes and an orange. And a 200 ml bottle of prune juice, another kitchen kickback.

'So what's up with your stiff, Puff?'

'Nothing, and that's the problem. A few clues which at this point are meaningless. You?'

'Oh, you know, the usual. Kids, ice, GHB and a supply chain that's breakable except we can't just go in and break. "Insufficient evidence",' she says, her laced sarcasm washed down with a slug of prune juice. She breaks a piece of the crumbly cheese onto a cracker, crunches.

I'm finished. I sit back, enjoying watching her.

'Want a meal tonight Franz? My place?'

'Sure. Not lamb kofta, though …'

My mobile rings.

'Heineken.'

43

'Mr Heineken, Knacker McConachie here.'

'Hello, Knacker. Got something for me?'

'Yeah. Well, a mate has. And it's just like you thought, Mr Singing Detective.'

'FAYE! LET'S GO, BRING YOUR NOTEBOOK.' I'M CHUCKING ON MY JACKET as I hurry into the corridor.

She chases after me and we take the steps to the basement at a fair clip. Here's how small Hobart is: it takes all of six minutes to exit Davey Square, cross the CBD and park in a loading zone near Manzini's Men's Hairdressers. By the standards of these joints it's big, having five chairs. And busy. Three grey-coated blokes cutting, two customers waiting, the tiled floor around the chairs a choppy sea of brown, black and grey hair tufts.

'Paolo Manzini?'

The youngest cutter looks at me. 'Yes?'

'Knacker sent me.'

'Moment.' He continues to cut, speeding up by the looks of things. The customer, if he notices, isn't commenting. And once their business is done and the payment made, Paolo Manzini ushers us into the back, through an open doorway hung with plastic coloured strips. There's a sink, a table, barber business stuff everywhere. I introduce myself, Faye, show my card. He gestures chairs and we sit. He's twenty-five if that. Apprehensive.

'You know why we're here, Paolo?'

'Si, yes. The dead one.'

Heavily accented. He can't have been here long.

'This your family business?'

'Uncle.'

'Good.' I take out the ID of the deceased, lay it down for him to have a good look. The loud T-shirt, the shoes, the shaved head. Again he nods, swallows. Faye's got her book out, pen working.

'What can you tell us about him?'

'See, is like this. So, ah …' He's calculating something. 'Fifteen days ago to this day, he walk in.' Paolo points at the fly strips. 'He walk in for a cut. He is, how to say, like a gringo, this same shirt, this same shoes, very long hair to his back, ponytail, long Mexican moustache, long sideburns, long, maybe not so long beard, pirate beard, but all joined, and he say, "Cut it off! Make me skinhead

44

again!" ' Paolo stops abruptly, eyes flicking from the image to me, to Faye, to the image again.

'Did he say why, Paolo?'

'He say he say he want the boys from the old club to, how you say …?' Paolo makes a vee with two fingers and points them at his eyes.

'To recognise him?'

'Si! Yes.'

' "The boys from the old club"? Those exact words?'

Paolo exhales noisily, winces, waggles one hand from side to side. It's a nice Italian gesture, but not what I want to see.

'I think yes, maybe. He say club because I think, soccer?'

'Did you ask him that?'

'No.'

'What did you talk about while you were cutting his hair?'

'He seem a happy man but not for talking. He just stare hard in the mirror as I cut and shave.'

'Did you get some idea of what he meant by "old"? How old?'

'He don't say. But his hair is got some grey, that hair growing for many years.'

'Were there other customers? Perhaps he talked to someone else?'

Young Manzini shakes his head. 'Only me here. First cut of the day. Is very quiet, eight o'clock in the morning.'

That's interesting too, as if he hadn't wanted an audience.

'Paolo, why are you only telling us this now?'

He nods. 'Si, understand. That same morning, my mother take ill. She live in Sicilia.'

'Sicily?'

'Si – Sicilia.'

'Sorry to hear it. So you went there?'

'Was terrible. My mother is dying and I am trying to get aeroplanes, very difficult, you know how it is.'

We nod sympathetically.

'On that day, get to Melbourne, wait wait wait. Then Singapore, wait, change. Zurich, wait, change. Roma, wait wait wait, change. Napoli, wait wait wait wait, change, Palermo, change, then drive nonstop my family town, Agrigento, you know how it is.'

I want to say yes, I do know how it is, I try to get to Agrigento whenever I can, but another nod will do.

Paolo sighs. 'She die.'

'I'm sorry.'

'I stay for the mourning, the funeral, help my little sister. I get back to Hobart one night before yesterday. Then Knacker, he ring.'

'That's good, Paolo. We'll need you to talk to a police artist, to make a new identikit picture, okay?' I point at the one on the table.

'Si.'

'I'd like you to come with us as soon as you can, please. It is important. Can you come now?'

He looks miserably at us. How much easier to just get back behind the scissors. 'Moment', he says, rising. Out he goes through the strips. We wait, Faye double checking her notes. Paolo returns. 'One hour?'

'Sure. I'll have a car waiting for you right outside.'

I don't mind. It might take that long to get one of our artists. Waiting customers, four of them, look up at us as we leave. Who are we? A pair of sinister Brylcreem salesmen, eh.

Out on the street Faye says, 'Fantastic.'

'Yes. The sweet science of bruising.'

'Beg pardon?'

'The pugilistic art.'

'*What?*'

We're at my car. I'm not a demonstrative person, but on this occasion I briefly hold up my arms and fists and adopt an old-fashioned Queensberry Rules boxing pose before her. 'Let's say long ago is twenty years ago and it was a sporting club. Sportsmen fancied their hairstyles back then. But not boxers. They've always only ever had skull shaves, or close to it.'

'You think so, sir?'

I shrug, unlock the vehicle, we get in, belt up, ease into the traffic.

'Don't know, Faye. How accurate is that young bloke's memory? When he said, "the boys from the old club", then waggled his bloody hand, I wanted to ask him to swear on it by his mother's grave, but under the circumstances ...'

LATE AFTERNOON. RAIN, WIND, SWOLLEN MOUNTAIN CLOUD. SAVAGE temperature plunge. A lamb kofta might have been good after all. Our new best friend Paolo's still with the identikit artist. The result better be good. It's too late for this evening's TV, and touch and go with the front page of even the Tassie morning newspapers. That will effectively put back its release twenty-four hours in the major news cycle.

Rafe sticks his head in the door. 'Just popping down for a Coke, boss. Can you intercept our phones if they ring?'

'Where's Faye?'

'Out and about on what you might call a key fact-finding mission. Visiting some old places in the city and New Town. She was a bit overexcited. But, y'know, young, she's that eager ... '

'Go and get your Coke.'

ONE OF THE THINGS ABOUT HEDDA IS THAT SHE'S A STRICT VEGETARIAN. It's not blood squeamishness. I've seen her deliver a fearsome *mawashageri*, a roundhouse kick, to a sparring partner in her *sensei*'s Bellerive dojo, unintentionally spraying the partner's facial claret all over the place. Nor is it a moral position. I haven't the faintest idea why she doesn't eat fish, fowl or beast, although I'm sure I once asked. But I do know she's not a fruitarian, which is one who will not pick, pluck or uproot live matter in order to consume it. The matter must first die naturally. So tonight I'm guessing that DS Andover will have thought about the lamb kofta snippet, and we'll be eating some smartarse vegetarian equivalent in her Battery Point flat. Which turns my mind to wine. A white and a red. I haven't had much of anything since coming back from the shack, no time, but maybe now's that time. Five minutes in a bottle shop looking for one white and one red to go with ...

Mobile. Mine. Faye.

'Boss! I've found it! I've found the door to the key!'

IT TAKES ME AND RAFE ALL OF EIGHT MINUTES IN THE COMMODORE TO exit Davey Square, cross the CBD and scream to a big cop halt in Campbell Street right outside the one place we, us, I, could have, should have, picked as a perfect den site for a transient fox, not that we want foxes in Tasmania. Smart Faye, once she made the match, stayed put, *in situ*, and now her boys are here. Her expression's one of pride, standing chest out in the old brick doorway of the place.

The Alexander Pearce Hotel is a seedy beige establishment clinging grimly to the edge of the CBD. Its low two storeys host an assortment of single residents and it takes in a few 'Prisdon Graduates', recently released felons with nowhere to go. The APH, a Hobart institution for decades, is dirt cheap and a stagger away from what was until recently a controlled touching bar, the pavements outside of which were a grey mosaic of piss and vomit stains. The APH is a grim joint but serves a useful social purpose, offering medium-term accommodation to single men.

How many times have I entered this place? A fair few. But I wouldn't have picked it for our victim because the place has no history of catering to blow-ins from the big island wearing fancy shirts and sharp reptilian footwear. Nor did the management respond to the identikit. Ah, not to the old one …

A young boofhead, unshaven and incongruous in a collar and tie, watches us from behind his reception corner tucked away in one dim corner. He can't hear us talking, but it's obvious he's trying. Faye hands me the key.

'Have you been to the room yet?'

'Yes.'

'You didn't want to wait for us?'

'I had to make sure.'

'What did you tell the fellow behind the counter?'

'Only that it's a police matter. He didn't want to believe that I'm a cop. The key's apparently supposed to have a tag on it with the room number, but he recognised it straight up.'

'So our corpse ripped the tag off.'

'I reckon,' Rafe says. 'Tickle the poor bloke's chest otherwise.'

'He came up with me to the room. I just unlocked the door, peeped so he couldn't see in, locked it again.'

'What's in there?'

'Not much that I saw.'

We walk to the reception counter. I flick my ID at the boofhead, and because I'm also the oldest and ugliest he focuses his attention fully on me.

'G'day,' he says, in the unblinking manner of his kind.

'Are you the manager?'

'No, mate. He won't be in 'til after six.'

'What's your name?'

'Brody.'

'Okay, Brody. The room that this key opens is now part of a formal crime investigation. You understand what that means?'

'Sort of, yeah.'

'It means that the room is out of bounds and that you, and anyone else associated with this place, will be obliged to answer any questions we may ask.'

'Yeah …' He looks doubtful. 'I'd better okay that with Hardo.'

'Hardo?'

'Proprietor, mate. Mr Hardwick. He won't want …'

'We'll get to him in a minute.' Just for emphasis, I wag the key at him. 'When did the occupant of this room check in?'

Boofhead no-shave Brody drags a slow, stubby finger down a column of a tatty registration book lying open on the table behind him. 'Room 21. He booked in on the fifteenth.'

'That's nearly two weeks ago, Brody. But he hasn't been in that room for ten days.'

'Hasn't he? Sorry, mate, I wouldn't know about that, I'm not here every day.'

'Well, who is he?'

Brody consults the book. 'Tom Jones.'

'Address?'

'Uhm … he just wrote "NSW". That'd be New South Wales.'

'No actual address? A phone number?'

'Sorry, mate.'

'No shit, Sherlock?' Rafe leans aggressively across the counter. 'That narrows the search down! Tom Jones of New South Wales! Brody, tell us, I don't suppose he's got big curly black hair, Welsh accent, great singing voice?'

'Dunno mate, wasn't me checked him in, but I can ask … '

I can't help rubbing a hand down my face. 'Did you see him at all, Brody?'

'No, mate. Well, I might've, but the blokes come and go here. It's their homes. I'm just here to check 'em in and out, and answer the phone.'

My patience is being sorely tested. Try again. 'Your residents have to pay in advance, don't they, Brody?'

'Yeah, otherwise none of 'em would pay at all! 'Cept for those who got agencies paying for 'em.'

'So you'll have a record of your Mister Tom Jones's payment.'

The finger trawls down the page. 'Bloke paid cash for two weeks. Fifty-five bucks a day. So he's still okay.'

'No, he's not okay. Give me a phone number for Mr Hardwick.'

Brody hands me a creased business card. Ronnie Hardwick, Prop. Alexander Pearce Hotel. He does business with it, alright. Centrelink, homeless men's networks, get out of jail not quite free. I flick it on to Rafe, who thumbs numbers into his mobile.

'We're going up to his room now, Brody. While we're there, you keep this conversation to yourself.' I favour him with an unpleasant, cold stare. 'Tell anyone, anyone at all, and I'll book you for disobeying a police instruction. Is that clear?'

'Yeah, hey. I won't be sayin nothin' to no one.'

'Show us, Faye.'

We walk across to the dingy flight of stairs, up to the first floor, Rafe tailing, and telling Hardwick in politely curt language to get here five minutes ago. By the sound of Rafe's voice, Hardwick, who's not known to me, tried objecting.

Faye stops at the door with a lopsided brass 21 screwed on it. The corridor smells of unwashed clothes and urinal fragrance balls, engaging with a subtle hint of old stew. I unlock the door, push it squeakily open. The room's small, dingy, functional. Single bed, bedside lamp table, cupboard, one plastic chair, a flimsy TV table, a basin in one corner alongside a closed sash window through which the tip of the Cenotaph is visible.

A crumpled copy of the *Mercury* on the bed. On the table, a suitcase, closed. A pair of thongs on the floor. Nothing else. We go carefully, so as to preserve what there is for FU, but the lack of mess, the lack of just about anything, suggests there won't be much for them.

Rafe peers down at the newspaper. 'The sixteenth,' he says. 'The day after he checked in.'

'Could be useful.'

The front page photo is of a US aircraft carrier. I was still at the shack when it anchored in the Derwent opposite Droughty Point, disgorging a few thousand clean-cut Marines into the city for their brief R&R.

Faye carefully opens the cupboard. Among the rusty wire hangers is a lightweight jacket. She feels the pockets. Nothing.

'Hey!' Rafe's turned the newspaper over. 'There's a phone number scribbled here.'

'Local?'

'Yep. Last number's a bit … Five. Or three …'

I push up the lid of the suitcase. Male clothes in a messy airless heap. Half a carton of cigarettes, two lighters. I feel among the clothes. Nothing. The inside lid of the suitcase has a mesh compartment, and inside this is a mess of used socks and underdaks. A shocking afterstench hits my face.

'Jesus!' Rafe grabs his nose.

I feel among the filthy garments. Withdraw a ball of socks. Inside them is a mobile phone. I hold it up between thumb and forefinger.

'Who would he be hiding it from?' Faye asks.

A short man materialises in the doorway.

'Mr Hardwick?'

'Yeah. What's up?'

He's made for the job. One dark liquid eye slightly squint, damp black hair spread thinly over a greasy bald spot, jowels, a chin dimple chipped out by hammer and screwdriver, sweaty, dirty collar, thin black tie, shiny black suit, clownishly pointy black shoes, and two fat shiny silver rings on two fat hairy fingers. He's looking apprehensively at us, as if we might confiscate the joint and jab lighted matchsticks under his fingernails.

'Come in Mr Hardwick. I've got some questions for you.'

I show him the much-publicised shaven ID of the deceased. He recognises it straight away, gives me a bit of a look, parts his lips and exhales a relieved, garlic-laden laugh.

'It's not him. That's someone else.'

'Then describe Mr Tom Jones for us.'

'Tallish, skinny, long ponytail, General Custer tash and sideboards. An old hippy, maybe a bikie.'

'They're one and the same person Mr Hardwick.'

'Ah, shit. Really?'

'Yeah, really,' Rafe says, 'absolutely bloody really!'

'We'll need to go through a formal interview process with you, Mr Hardwick, at police headquarters. The sooner the better.'

'Like, now? I take over from Brody at six, plus I always gotta watch over the kitchen staff.' He's looking anxiously at me. I can understand his desire not to have to break his routine at such short notice. He is, after all, in a position of some responsibility. But there's no way I'm giving him a night to think about it, if by chance there's something he mightn't want to reveal.

'Yes, now. This is a murder investigation.'

He frowns at his watch, sighs fretfully. 'I'll get Brody to stay. Bloke's not a maths Olympian, but …'

'Faye, we'll need a uniform here twenty-four seven until further notice, and the sooner FU can get someone through the better.'

'Okay.' She uses her mobile, leaves the room. Sensible kid, the air's almost normal out there. Rafe kneels, peers under the bed.

'Just one thing Mr Hardwick. Brody has told us that your residents and guests come and go, sometimes for days at a time, and that it's none of your business if they're mysteriously awol. That's fair enough. But I also know that you checked Mr Tom Jones in. So how much did you speak with him while he was here? Notice anything unusual?'

'Bloke was cashed up, for starters.'

'How?'

'When he checked I said, you gotta pay in advance, how long do you plan to stay, it's fifty-five a night. Well, he brought out a wallet full of green ones and counted out eight, and he said, in that case mate give me two weeks. I said, okay, and I owe you thirty change, and he said, don't worry about it. We don't get many such guests.'

'You comment on his generosity?'

Hardwick shakes his head. 'Not my business.'

'I can tell you, Mr Hardwick, that he stayed in this room at least until the eighteenth. That's four days. There must have been something else you noticed about him in that time.'

'Not me as such. But one of my permanents complained.'

'About what?'

'That he and another bloke made a shitload of noise one night.'

'What other bloke? A guest?'

'Yeah.'

'What kind of noise?' Rafe asks. Hardwick turns his greasy attention to him. 'Uh … dunno for sure, just loud. But the funny thing is, the other bloke shot through early next morning. Left his key at reception, room empty, even though he'd paid through to the weekend.'

'Is that so Mr Hardwick? Well then, let's cross our fingers and hope you've got some proper contact details for him downstairs.'

'And I'll tell you this for free,' Rafe adds, 'if he's Mick Jagger of Mildura you're deep in the poo, mate.'

'HEY, THERE YOU ARE.'

'Sorry I'm late.'

'Who are you seeing? Is that lipstick on your collar? Where's my rolling pin?'

'It's who I've seen. Let me in, I'm buggered and thirsty.'

'I can see that.' Hedda gives me a kiss, leads me into her groovy pad, her top floor Battery Point apartment. 'There, there,' she says, 'I'll fix everything for poor Franz. Cold beer, warm chick, hot tucker waiting in the oven. What more could an underworked, overpaid crime dick want?'

I laugh at that, park on a kitchen bar stool. She opens me a Boags Premium, replenishes her Bream Creek riesling.

'Cheers, Andover.'

'Tables.'

We clink our stubby and flute. Her place has a fine view over the yacht club. In summer, with the windows open at night, the tinkling of masts is a background music. That and the pissed laughter of yachties. I lean back as far as I judge safe on the stool, stretch kinks out of my lower back, shoulders, neck.

'Nice smell.'

'Me?'

'And from the oven.'

'Lamb kofta.'

'You don't cook meat, remember?'

'Okay, you win. Imam bayildi, havuc kizartmasi, and beyaz pilav.'

It's a game we play from time to time. When Hedda makes it her business to cook something, she's good at it.

'Turkish?'

'Well done Franz! Stuffed eggplant, carrot fritters, pine nut pilaf. Should be tops with a heavy-duty red. Anyway, why the overtime? Don't tell me you're sucking up to Walter.'

'Breakthroughs, Andover, falling out of today's sky. Our dead bloke's taken on a new look. He was like a Mexican bandido, and he was staying at the Alexander Pearce Hotel when – not where, when – he got slugged. Registered there under an alias. He waved money about, and he seems to have got involved in some kind of argy bargy with a fellow guest. The name of that guest is Athol Burden. We've traced him to a property near Deloraine. He, Burden, cut short his stay at the APH by four days, even though he'd paid for them. He skipped the hotel on the day el signor Tom Jones karked it. Best of all, Athol Burden is a registered shooter. He culls crop browsers for farmers, feral dogs, cats, goats, you name it. A professional Tasmanian wild animal shooter.'

I'm drained. Whacked. I savour a long slug of the ice cold lager frequently voted the world's best.

'The deer bag?' she asks. 'The type of rifle that killed him?'

I nod. 'And we found a mobile phone in the dead bloke's suitcase. It's got one unregistered number stored in it. Nothing else. That mobile was one of a Nokia batch sold from Sydney outlets about five years ago. Oh, and just to keep you from dozing off, there's also a telephone number he scribbled down. A local number, Hedda. Guess what it is, now that I've given you the sketch of the type of customers we're dealing with.'

She thinks through a generous slug of wine. 'Give up. Spill the beans.'

'The Dynnyrne Child Care Centre. Where Hobart's finest send their spoilt brats.'

'You're kidding.'

I shake my weary, satisfied scone. Hedda eyes me off, grins.

'Oh, mate, is this one growing legs or what!'

6

NOT ONLY DOES HEDDA GIVE GOOD TURKISH, SHE KNOWS HOW TO select her reds. So I'm feeling a bit grim in the 8 am strategy meeting in Hunt's lair.

Goody Two Shoes, alias Chief Super Walter D'Hayt, is looking sickeningly well. Present also, by video hook-up, is DI Jim Joyce, my Launceston equivalent, Deloraine being part of his patch.

Hunt nods at me. 'Take us through a plan of action, Franz.'

'We have four leads, four potential sources of information. An accurate identikit, a mobile phone, the child care centre connection and Athol Burden. The new ID is passive. We have to wait, see what it brings. The mobile phone may be difficult to track. It's been wiped and the number stored in it is unregistered.'

'Professional criminals,' Walter says.

We all pretty much assume that, but it's hardly surprising Walter voices it, so accustomed is he to taking any opportunity to earn brownie points.

'So we move on the other two straight away. Jim, what can you tell us about this Burden character?'

I like Jim Joyce. Ironic, in its way, that I sunk the fangs into Walter for trying to shift Faye onto Jim. He's an unlikely major crime cop, gangly, and with a mild and vaguely apologetic expression. He'd look perfect with an organic vegetable in each hand rather than a Glock and a villain's mugshot.

'Forty-eight, married, no children, an acreage south of Deloraine. He's been a registered shooter for twenty years, so he's well known to the people who use his services, the farmers, horticulturalists, local councils. He's a cleanskin, though he did pay a fine some years ago for shooting deer out of season. Parks and Wildlife people say he's reliable. That's a bit surprising because the word is he gets seriously on the piss. Routine seems to be he goes bush for weeks at a time, doing one or more jobs. Gets back to civvy street, parties.'

'So he's got drinking mates?'

'Not sure. I received this anecdotally. If he's got a social circle, I'll know about it soon enough.'

Jim's face and shoulders begin to pixilate and his voice cuts out briefly. Technology you can trust.

'Say again, Jim.'

'… And I can confirm he uses deer bags. He's constantly carting animal corpses in the course of his work. The feral dogs and cats he's supposed to burn or bury, the marsupials and deer end up as pet food. Oh, and while he's a not a big fella he's well used to humping sacks of meat around. Like the little blokes who do those amazing clean and jerks at the Olympics.'

'Got the picture, Jim,' Hunt says. 'It's a good start. For mine, he's well in the frame, given there's so little else to go on. Franz, tell Jim about the circumstances of the complaint at the hotel.'

'It was made to the proprietor, Hardwick, by a permanent resident, an old fellow, senility's coming on. Wouldn't make him an ideal witness, but he was animated when I spoke to him yesterday evening. He said that the deceased was in Burden's room, next to his own, and that he couldn't sleep because they were shouting. At one point he banged on the door, and our dead man opened it. He then still had the hair. The room was in semi-darkness and the old bloke copped a blast. He said a girl was with them. He was told to piss off and mind his own business. So he went downstairs and whinged to Hardwick. When I asked Hardwick about it yesterday evening he confirmed that he'd taken no action because the old man complained a lot and because he didn't want to upset his cashed-up guest. He gave the old man a glass of cooking sherry and told him to sleep it off.'

'A senile serial complainer,' Walter says doubtfully. 'A defence lawyer will chew that up and spit it out.'

'Walter, sorry, but my focus has to be narrower than a possible trial months away. It's sufficient witness evidence to put them together and make Burden a person of interest.'

'I reckon,' Jim adds. 'Plus we'll be giving him the opportunity to clear himself.'

'So here's my calculation to this point: the deceased checked into the hotel and bought the *Mercury*, though he didn't necessarily scribble the child care centre's number on it that day. On the third night he was in

Burden's room. Burden left early the next morning, four days before he was due to check out. The deceased had his hair cut by Paolo Manzini that day, and on the same day, or the one after, he was murdered.'

'Okay. What about the child care centre? That's a puzzle.' Hunt sits back and laces his fingers.

'He could have scribbled the number down incorrectly. And of course we don't know whether he got it from directory services or an associate of some kind. The centre itself is a busy place. On the three days he could have rung they took upward of seventy calls each day from 8 am to 6 pm. The data on the originating numbers is still being crunched and that will take some time. I do know that most incoming calls are parents. One possibility is that he was associated with a planned abduction that didn't eventuate, either a domestic or for financial gain.'

'An interstate gun for hire?' Hunt says. 'I don't like that. And such speculation doesn't leave this room. But I agree, it's hard otherwise to consider a link. What do you propose, then, Franz?'

'To visit the centre this morning and talk to staff, and –'

Walter interrupts, 'Who are you taking with you?'

'Faye Addison.'

'Good.'

'Rafe Tredway's trying to get a trace on the mobile, and he'll do Burden with me. Jim, I'm hoping you can get some more on him before we pull him in later this afternoon. Assuming he's at home. Rafe and I will drive up as soon as I've done the people at the child care centre.'

'Sounds good, mate. I'm on the case.'

'Excellent. See you later, Jim.' Hunt stands briskly. No time for small talk. Full day ahead.

'THIS IS ALL VERY MYSTERIOUS, BUT I DO HOPE I CAN HELP.' SUSAN Sohks, Director of the Dynnyrne Child Care Centre, ushers Faye and me into her office. It has a nice view of the mountain. It also has a god's eye view, down through a large angled glass structure, of the centre's main playroom. They would have paid top dollar for a trendy architect to come up with it. Ms Sohks wears specs with a drop-down cord, not currently in use, and dangly earrings. She's far too tall for a toddler to take a swipe at them. And she has about her an air of considerable efficiency.

We sit, I talk. 'Ms Sohks, we're here in connection with the individual who was found murdered at Outer North Head. We have reason to believe that he may have made a phone call to this centre not long before he died.'

Her eyebrows shoot up behind the specs and her mouth drops open. '*What?*'

'We've narrowed the potential time for this call to a period of three days. You should know that we will be looking at the centre's phone records for those days.'

She nods, trying to get a grip on it. A murdered hooligan buried on a remote beach and her darling little ones safely here in care. We can see some of them even now assembling in front of a plasma TV and the bright pastels of *Playschool*. 'But how do you know, Inspector?'

'He wrote your number down. The first and obvious question is, can you think of any reason why such an individual might want to contact your centre? To talk to a staff member, for instance?'

'Well, I'm absolutely stunned, and the answer to that question is an emphatic no. There are nine of us who work here, full-time or part-time, and we've been together for years. It's just unthinkable that one of us would somehow – I mean, *yuk! No!*' She emits a strangled, horrified sort of laugh. Very Dynnyrne, I imagine, whereas her counterparts in the outer northern suburbs would be taking it on the chin and reaching for the client list.

'What about the parents? Any signs of distress or something out of the ordinary recently with a parent?'

'Again, no. I mean, why on Earth would such a person want anything to do with *us?*'

'That's why we're here, Ms Sohks.'

'Of course ...'

'Perhaps you could arrange for Detective Constable Addison and me to talk to your staff. A few minutes each should be fine. Routine, but it must be done. Is there a room we can use?'

'Yes, this office, since I'll need to be on deck. If the phone rings ignore it, one of us will answer it at the reception desk. Oh but hang on, you'll only be able to talk to four of us this morning. Most of the kids are at the Singing Sugar Gliders concert in the Town Hall.'

That seems to stress her more, as if she's erected a barrier, but it'll suit me to process who's here and then get on with the Athol Burden side of the day. Faye can do the rest of her staff this afternoon. And the fact is, it's the Director I wanted to hear from. She'd surely have connected our visit to a problem if there'd been one.

'Didn't you notice we have very few children here today? Just the littlies.'

'I did.' Faye smiles broadly at her. Susan Sohks takes it as some kind of compliment. I take it as a rookie plainclotheser doing her job, noticing when the obvious is missing – not always as straightforward as it seems.

'Alright, Ms Sohks, if you wouldn't mind.' I gesture her at her door. She gives me a peculiar, dissatisfied look, full of earring tossing. I return it, minus the latter. Someone associated with this place is also associated with murder and I want to find out who.

'THREE DOWN, ONE TO GO. WHAT DO YOU THINK, FRANZ?'

'As expected.' I look at my watch. Come on ...

Susan Sohks, down there on her deck, seems to run a tight ship, because the staff we've spoken to have been as gobsmacked as she was at the reason for our visit. For Faye this is a good experience. Interviewing 'the public' is generally much more miss than hit, with recollections of events or individuals ranging from faulty through reasonable to wildly exaggerated. I've even had cases of phantom recollection, when members of the public in all honesty describe events they could not possibly have witnessed. One of our psychologists reckons it's likely to be the uncovering of a deeply retained image from TV, a cop drama or reality series. Be that as it may, I wasn't impressed with Susan's deputy who, and she meant it as a compliment, likened us to characters from *The Bill*.

Susan enters her office with a woman in her mid-forties, pale blue jeans, rubber-soled brown shoes, shirt. Short brown hair, fringe, attractive. Not least because of her almond-shaped Queen Nefertiti eyes, and is it just the old Pufferfish nose or is she leaking unease?

'This is Debbie Hart, Inspector. Debbie runs the ship! She's our cleaner, maintenance whizz and cook all rolled into one!' Susan leans slightly towards her. 'They say it'll just take a few minutes, dear. I'll do the pikelets.'

'Hello, Debbie. This is Detective Constable Faye Addison.'

Debbie sits opposite us. Her large eyes are clear and blue and hold mine in an ever so fragile gaze. I sit.

'You'll know why we're here, Debbie.'

'Yes.'

She swallows. Can't help it.

I wait. Faye, in my peripheral vision, is rigid in her seat.

'How, how, horrible.' Debbie Hart flicks at her fringe with a minutely trembling hand.

'Would you know anything about it?'

Debbie Hart chuckles. Sort of. But she has expelled some of whatever it is trapped inside her. 'Me? Just what I've read and seen on TV. It's just so …' She looks down, then up at Faye. 'I hope you get whoever did it.'

'We will,' Faye says.

'Debbie, you seem upset. Is there anything you need to tell us?'

She frowns lightly at me. A smidgeon of confidence restored. 'About the murder? No way! It's just so ghastly, that's all.'

'Sure. Do you answer the phone here much?'

'The phone? Uhm … sometimes … I mean we all do.'

'Did you take a strange call about two weeks ago?'

She purses her lips, thinks about it. We watch her thinking about it. Then Debbie Hart shakes her head. 'Sorry, no.'

'Unusual, isn't it,' I muse, 'how that sort of bad behaviour can be linked to a child care centre.'

Debbie doesn't answer. Not that she has to.

'Well, Debbie, that's your piece of reality TV. Thanks for your time.'

She stands, laughing at me. Either I'm a great wit or she's bloody relieved.

'Good luck,' she says, turning on us and walking soundlessly out in her sensible cleaner's shoes. She closes the door behind her. I look through the door, wondering vaguely if a place of toddlers and diminutive runabouts should have so much glass. A bare few minutes ago Faye had asked me what I thought so far. She was making conversation, really. Whereas now I really want to know what *she* thinks. Hence, I'm not saying a word, just looking through that door at the departed Debbie Hart.

Faye makes a little whistling sound.

'Oh my God, she knows something.'

I nod.

'I mean, boss, it's just so *obvious*.'

'How?'

She doesn't immediately answer. Welcome to major crime, Det. Const. Addison.

7

JIM JOYCE WAS RIGHT ABOUT ATHOL BURDEN IN THIS RESPECT: HE'S A nugget. And in the few hours since our strategy meeting this morning Jim has uncovered another useful piece of information for me. Rafe and I are in Launceston HQ Interview Room No. 1, opposite Burden and a young legal aid lawyer, Jemima Carver. Burden's been in the lock-up for an hour, waiting for us to arrive. He's not happy, and the noticeably stunning Ms Carver has let us know that her client has every right not to cooperate, not being charged with anything. Still, here we all are, in a room into which late afternoon sunshine filters through chunky frosted glass.

Athol Burden is a true son of the soil. Black-and-red check shirt, rough khaki work pants, near-busted Blunnies – so they've still about five years in them. Square jaw, home-cut hair, sun-narrowed eyes and crinkled skin with fawn-brown cancers scattered across beefy forearms and the backs of stubby hands. Thick fingernails blunt with outdoor business. Formidable biceps under the rolled shirtsleeves. The way he walked in, flanked by a uniform and Ms Carver, he clearly takes pride in his physique. Short, but full of it.

He sits back, arms folded, seething. 'You blokes better have a bloody good reason for this.'

By way of answer Rafe holds up a hand, then switches on the tape, advises it who's present, date, time. 'Now you can say that again, mate,' he says to Burden. Just to warm us all up a bit more. Rafe's wearing what he calls his 'mean' interview gear, his black suit, dark purple shirt and black tie.

'Athol Burden,' I begin, 'you've been advised that we want to talk to you in connection with the discovery of the body at Outer North Head.'

'Yeah, that's what they said when they picked me up, and I told them, *nothing* to do with me! Mate, you can't just pull a bloke out of his house!'

'We have reason to believe that you were with the deceased shortly before he died.'

His look of disbelief seems genuine, and then he laughs at me. Funny, he's not the first one to do that today. Then to the lawyer he says, 'I'm glad you're here to listen to this tripe, love. They're full of it, aren't they?'

Full of it we may be, but we're also full of authority and there's nothing cranky Athol can do about that.

'Where is your evidence?' Ms Carver asks me.

No need to answer her. Not yet, at any rate.

'Mr Burden, do you deny staying at the Alexander Pearce Hotel earlier this month?'

That works. It's accusatory, and, like multiple choice, he's got to answer one way or the other, quickly. He is quick, though, while absorbing the shock of it.

'No. I was there. Why?'

'Why were you there?'

' 'Cause it's a flippin' hotel! I work bloody hard in the bush and I like to relax from time to time.' For emphasis, he waves his arms about.

'Why that particular hotel?'

Ms Carver, unless she was born yesterday, must know that I'm rolling my pastry thin. Indeed, she flashes me a look that says so. But she doesn't seem prepared to give the prickly one a serve this early in the piece.

'It's in the middle of Hobart. It doesn't cost much. And it wasn't full of American sailors.' Burden folds his arms again. Jemima Carver nods. She's had so little notice to represent him that she's probably hearing this for the first time.

'So you tried to book into other hotels?' Rafe asks.

'No. Why the bloody hell *should* I?'

'Hey, hey, chill, matey,' Rafe says equably, holding up his palms. 'Did you take a negative tablet this morning?'

Burden glares at him. He's filthy.

'Mr Burden, do you recognise this man?' I take out the skinhead ID and lay it on the table, nice and evenly spaced between he and his legal rep. He sighs.

'No! Well, yes, from just about every bloody newspaper and TV channel for the past two weeks. But do I otherwise "recognise" him? No, dammit!' And he bounces on his chair, looking at Ms Carver, wanting out.

'Then how about this man?' Card-like, neatly laid down on the table, alongside the old one, the new ID, the ponytail, the exuberant playful moustache, the sideboards – our wickedly hairy just as dead bloke.

Athol Burden stares down at it. 'Who's he?'

'Answer my question.'

'Uh – yeah, that bloke was there ... at the hotel ... Jesus, are you saying *he* killed him?'

'Under some circumstances I might find that kind of comment funny, Mr Burden, but not today. Those two' – I point at the IDs with vertical V-fingers, *à la* Paolo Manzini – 'are the same man.'

'Mate, no, can't be ...'

'So tell us about your association with him.'

'That's out of order!' Ms Carver sticks a protectively long arm across the table. 'What do you mean by "association", Inspector Heineken? You must provide evidence for making such a statement.'

'Did you talk to him, Mr Burden?'

Now the poor fellow has to choose between her and me. Would you prefer to hitch your star to a Saab or a steamroller, eh?

'Yeah, as it happens I did. Crime in that?'

'No. Where did you talk?'

'We went to a pub ... Jesus, poor bastard. Why was he killed?'

'What pub?' Rafe asks.

'Uhh ... some place on, what is it, Elizabeth Street?'

'Can you describe it?'

'Mate, sorry, at night – I don't live in Hobart ...'

'How often were you together?' Rafe asks.

'Just once, like I told you.'

'Did you walk together from the hotel to this pub?'

'Uhh ... guess so.'

'That's not very clear, Athol.'

'I can't be clearer.' Sits back, waves then refolds folds the chunky arms. Testing my offsider.

Rafe stands, stretches his back. 'Did you associate with hi – sorry, did you *talk* to him at the hotel?' He takes a few paces away, swings about so as to view Burden anew, plants his legs wide, aggressively sticks his fists on his hips, elbows jutting. Whack reflective sunnies and black boot polish on my Det. Tredway and he's President-for-life Akimbo of the Dark Continent.

'Can't remember, mate.'

'Dumb answer, mate.'

Jemima Carver leaps up. 'You can't say that to my client!'

'But I did – love.'

Apoplectic anger stills her tongue. Like bad fire conditions, where high temperatures, low humidity and dry growth meet, results are combustible. Rafe looks at Jemima. Jemima looks at Rafe. No love lost there. Athol Burden's suddenly out of his league. Who are these people from nowhere and hell this afternoon?

My turn to right the ship. 'Mr Burden, we all now know that you socialised with this man. But are there facts that you are keeping from me?'

'Nuthin'.'

'Did this man come into your room at the Alexander Pearce Hotel?'

'No.'

'You're sure?'

'Yes.'

'You paid in advance to stay at the hotel?'

'Yes.'

'For how many nights?'

'Aw, couldn't remember right off.'

'Try.'

'Three?'

'You paid in advance to stay at the hotel for seven nights, Mr Burden. You vacated your room after three nights. Why?'

'Got sick of it. Went home.'

'Like a shortened holiday?'

'Yeah, call it that.'

'No other reason?'

'No.'

'Mr Burden, I may look stupid. I may even sound stupid. But I am not, however, stupid. I have court-acceptable evidence, that is to say uncontestable witness statements, to prove that you and the deceased were in close proximity in that hotel, that the two of you may have been in violent conflict in that hotel, and that –'

She's up again, and I can't blame her. It's outrageous of me to bring the 'V' word in – but then, Athol Burden now looks as if he's got no objection at all, because the poor bloke's sagging, as if his pecs have developed slow punctures.

Time for a pause. We're all sitting in our various guises, thinking. If there were big clock hands on the wall of this unfriendly room, they might be stuck, favouring none. For myself, it's another few moments in a very long career. I therefore ease back slightly, little brown bag out of jacket pocket. I take out a pink, yellow and black liquorice allsort, so that the company knows what's in the bag. I stick the allsort between my teeth, offer the bag's contents to Athol Burden. He says no, by, in a way, shaking his eyes, so bitterly cruel is the offer. Ms Carver doesn't want one either. Rafe I don't offer because he doesn't eat them.

All square then. Ms Carver has subsided.

'Mr Burden?'

'There was no violence.'

'Why did you leave the hotel early?'

'I was embarrassed.'

'About what?'

Athol Burden looks woefully at his young legal aid helper, then at me, then Rafe, then down at his wide khaki legs on their chair. He wants to dive straight through cement and solid earth and leave us all behind in this nightmare of his own making.

'Sir, I didn't kill him. Please?'

'Answer the question.'

'We went in my room with a girl.'

'There's nothing wrong with that!' Ms Carver says, to all of us.

'What happened with the girl?'

'Just like you'd expect. It was gonna be sex. But not how they wanted it to be …'

'No threats, no violence?'

'No!'

'We'll obviously need to talk to her.'

'Jeez, well …' He brightens. 'She gave us her card.' He pats his shirt, as if it might magically be on his person.

'Her card?'

'Yeah, she said she's a sex worker down for the sailors' trade.'

Fair enough. Sex workers do descend on Hobart at such times. 'Her name, Mr Burden?'

'Uh … Kim.'

'That's not much to go on. Big country.'

'Her card said she works for an agency called something like, uhm, Lip Service?'

'Melbourne? Sydney?'

'Sydney.'

Jemima Carver looks brighter too and I don't blame her. Athol Burden sees it and shifts in his seat, not quite as queasy-faced as a minute ago.

'Tell us what happened?'

'She, this Kim, she knew him.'

'What, like friends? He's her pimp?'

'No. Yes, friends.'

'And?'

'Look, I reckon Stan set it all up. He wanted me in as a third party.'

'He called himself Stan? Stan who?'

Carver stares meaningfully at me. How little *do* I know?

'Just Stan.'

'Set it up so …?'

'She said, "Boys, I gotta have both of you together, I'm a cockaholic." I was havin' none of that, thanks. Pissed me off good, and he and me had a bit of a disagreement.'

'How?'

'Push came to shove. She was my girl. He, y'know, said three of us. Mate, I was ready to belt him, but just got out of there instead.'

'So you were annoyed. But why cut short your holiday, for which you'd paid good money?'

'Look, I just didn't want to see him next day, okay?'

'We know that you stay in Hobart at least once a year and you've been doing that for many years. But you've always stayed in mid-range hotels. Why this one, now?'

'Like I told you, sailors. And cheap.'

'You had no knowledge that Stan would be there?'

'None.'

'Alright … Let's go back a few steps. How exactly *did* you meet him?'

'Just bumped into each other.'

'In the hotel?'

'Yeah.'

'And then what?'

'We went on the piss.'

'Quick bonding, that.'

'If you like. No law against it.'

'No, there isn't. So what did you and Stan talk about?'

'Aw, y'know. Stuff. The usual. He was interested in me line of work.'

'What about his line of work?'

'Don't recall, to be honest.'

Rafe snorts. 'Come on, Athol, that's way not good enough. You and he become instant mates, you tell him all about yourself, but he's a blank page?'

'I swear to ya. He told me he's a Sydneysider, likes bikes, and he's thinking of relocating to Tassie. So that's why I did most of the talking. About Tassie.'

'And about yourself.'

'Yeah, a bit. Then the girl recognised him and came over.'

'Did he tell you why he wanted to come and live here?'

'Not that I recall.'

'What's he do for a crust?'

'Didn't say.'

'Unemployed?'

'Look, he didn't tell me!'

'Or he did and you conveniently forget?'

Athol Burden looks up at the daylight coming through the frosted glass and exhales. I wait for an answer but it's not forthcoming.

'Selective amnesia is never a good look, Mr Burden.'

'You can't make that inference,' Jemima Carver advises me. 'If he can't remember, he can't remember.'

'His memory of the events is otherwise reasonably good, wouldn't you say?'

Her jaw tightens. To Burden she says, 'You don't have to be forced into making an answer.'

He nods. And it's just about over for now. We don't have enough to hold him. He'll be pleased and so will she. But there's one more thing to keep him on his toes.

'Mr Burden, I take it you'll have no objection to providing us with fingerprints and DNA samples?'

'You don't have to,' she advises him. He frowns. Decisions, decisions. Great aureoles of sweat line his shirt from armpit to waist. He wants out, badly. And saying no won't help his case much.

'Yeah, right,' he says reluctantly. 'What do I have to do?'

'Don't worry, mate, we'll show you,' Rafe says, smiling broadly. Ms Carver and her client don't return the good cheer. 'And,' he adds just as cheerfully, "I don't know about you guys, but I could murder a Big Mac.'

RAFE AND I DON'T TALK MUCH ON THE DRIVE BACK TO HOBART. I'M NOT big on words at the best of times and Rafe isn't one who feels the need to fill empty space with empty rhetoric. And neither of us are satisfied with the Burden interview. Yes, it has holes in it and Tom Jones is now apparently Stan. But there's no motive. Without that we've got very little, make that nothing, and it leaves us feeling flat.

8

THE NOBLE TRADITION OF THE AUSTRALIAN SICKIE CAME UNDER SERIOUS assault back in the 1990s and it has never really recovered. I'm not sure this has been good for our nation. Absenteeism can put some serious zing in your Duracells, and I'm willing to bet that on balance a sickie is healthy. Just as my old pal Magnus will tell anyone within cooee that the time spent on working out GST calculations, being five per cent of a business owner's time, where previously it was nought, costs the nation a few billion each year in lost productivity. But it is the concept of the sickie that is occupying my mind this morning. On my way to work a call from HQ: please divert urgently to the Dynnyrne Child Care Centre.

No problem in that. My route from South Hobart conveniently enables me to swing right into Antill Street through the Video City-Hungry Jacks-Globe Hotel intersection, down the bendy incline and across the invisible Sandy Bay Rivulet. The thing about Dynnyrne is that as suburbs go it's mixed, from ultra expensive CBD-edge old piles to dirt-cheap student digs to modern credit boom extravagance hanging off the hillsides. With, it must be said, a green, tucked-in mountainside flavour. Not surprisingly the DCCC is slap bang in the middle of Dynnyrne's most upmarket enclave. And as I find a park alongside its friendly playgym, the intensity and subsequent deflation of the Burden interview makes it feel strange that it was also only yesterday that Faye and I were here. So what's up, eh?

Susan Sohks is waiting for me inside the expansive foyer, but off to one side so that the dribs and drabs of parents depositing their loved little ones don't bail her up for a chat. She only has eyes for Pufferfish. No one's dead or hurt or otherwise in danger, but you wouldn't know it from the fevered state of her.

'Oh thank God you're here Inspector, come with me.'

She marches, I follow, through a cheerful yellow door into a toddler room of legless leather and plastic block furnishings, where she points dramatically at an outsized *Sesame Street* clock on the floor surrounded by shards of splintered plastic. Then her point curves up to a bent hook high on the wall.

'See? I saw that the clock had stopped. These big ones are only battery operated. So I stupidly got up on that pouffe and unbalanced and, well, of course down it came, and ...' On she marches into a corridor. I can almost imagine spittle at the lips. '... to get the vacuum, because Debbie had just called in sick. And I went into her cleaning room and the vacuum bag was full, so of course I – I mean it's her world, she's so efficient we none of us *ever* need to go in here – couldn't find a new bag ... got up on a stool and felt into the back of the, the broomy vacuumy cupboard place, and – *oh!*'

We turn into a room off the corridor, strictly away from juvenile access. The cleaning room. Just a reasonably sized square space, with its far end being floor-to-ceiling cupboards containing the cleaning gear you would expect. What makes this room different is that on the middle of its floor is a child's yellow Bananas in Pyjamas backpack, unzipped, and much of the rest of the floor is covered in Australian bank notes, exclusively fifties and hundreds, the pale green ones predominating. A shallow sea of dollars. I look at them, marvelling. Susan Sohks, not being in the crime caper, has no such leverage. Her hands and long fingers are over her mouth and nose as she witnesses this appalling breach, betrayal, of everything she stands for.

It makes me gently cup her pointed elbow in the palm of my hand, until she looks sideways at me, then full on, horrified. Her eyes plead with mine. What can I do to erase this horror?

JUST OCCASIONALLY, OF COURSE, CHUCKING A SICKIE MASKS MORE THAN a desire to abstain briefly from the workplace. We spooked Debbie Hart yesterday and now we know why. Is the money connected to Stan née Tom Jones? Almost certainly. I've collected Faye on my way through the city and now we're lane-jumping our way to the eastern shore suburb of Bellerive, lights flashing. Crawling inbound rush-hour traffic clogs three of the bridge's narrow lanes. I'm conscious of heads turning as we shoot up and over the apex of the ribbony structure that was once felled by an iron ore tanker. Why the rush? She called in sick, just under an hour ago, but that doesn't mean she's lying wanly in bed with a hottie and a steaming mug of Lemsip.

She's forty-five. She's married to an accountant and they have a young adult daughter. She's been an employee of the DCCC for twelve years with an impeccable record of service. Before that she cleaned government offices at night. End of story of Debbie Hart. Until now.

We pull up outside a bland suburban house in Red Ochre Street. Her garden is noticeably well-tended. A blue Hyundai is at rest in the driveway. So she's home then, I'd seen the vehicle in the car park alongside the playgym yesterday morning. Hubby, presumably, has oiled into work in the CBD. Perhaps his was one of the heads turning on the bridge. Their daughter? I have no idea. But, now that we're here, Faye knows what to do. Nothing, basically, except to recall with certainty whatever Debbie Hart might say before we take her in for formal questioning.

I have reasonable grounds to arrest her without a warrant. We have so many different powers of arrest in Tasmania that law reformers are urging their reduction and codification, but just now I still have this option, and I'll take it if necessary. I knock. A pair of leadlight panes, black and red, are set into the upper panels of the door. Nice touch, but they prevent the occupant from knowing who the caller is and her shock at opening the door to us is almighty. In fact she all but says *Oh my God!* and a hand flies to her mouth as if to clamp it shut.

'Hello, Debbie, you'll remember us from yesterday.'

'Hello …'

Jeans, T-shirt, jumper, socks, freshly applied make-up. She's not unwell. Wasn't, until she answered the doorbell.

'May we come in? I've received some important information that you may be able to help us with.'

A large black cat strolls out the door. 'Get back inside Squizzy!' she says with a fair degree of emotion. Cats being cats, Squizzy saunters on, rubs itself against Faye's leg. What's wrong with the leg of Pufferfish, then?

Debbie, wordless, steps aside. We enter a passageway, move past her and along into a neat, orderly, characterless lounge-room. Everything's in it that should be, and in its place, but nothing remotely expresses the personalities of the occupants. It's odd. But what do I know about these people and their lives? Diddly squat. Faye and I stand together in the middle of the room. Debbie Hart is obliged to walk around us, turns to face us.

'Is something wrong?'

'Yes. What can you tell me about the yellow Bananas in Pyjamas backpack in your cleaning cupboard in the child care centre?'

She doesn't say anything. Can't. These moments are always tough, very difficult to grasp as the tremendous reality sets in. Caught out! Gotcha! For Faye, a front-seat novelty she'll get used to in time.

Debbie Hart puts her hands over her face. Her words are muffled.

'He asked me to look after it.'

'Why?'

'Because it wouldn't have been safe in that hotel.'

'Call a uniform car, would you please Faye? Mrs Hart will need to be taken under guard to HQ for questioning.'

'Will do, sir.' She wheels about and walks away. Debbie hasn't moved her hands. When she does, I see her tears, her quivering mouth, the stark off-white pallor of her face. Pure, unadulterated shock it is, and suddenly she cartwheels away, spews onto the once-soulless grey carpet. She makes a grating, choking sound, heaves and spews again. Faye instinctively wants to help her. I hold out an arm – uh-uh. Let her throw it all up. And until we know as many facts as we can about this mess, she's getting no favours, not while I'm looking for a killer or two.

THE FIRST PUBLIC RESPONSES TO THE ID OF STAN THE ENCHILADA-munching Zapatista have come in and they're good. But for now the three of us are in an interview room at Davey Square. Debbie's still a bit pale, and wearing a coat in place of the jumper, the sleeve of which she'd used to wipe her mouth and chin. She didn't want a lawyer. She said she just wanted to tell us everything. Tape's running. She's got her hands around a big friendly old HQ mug of steaming tea, into which she's staring blankly.

'Okay, Debbie, talk. Start wherever you think appropriate. There's no rush.'

'First of all, I want to, to apologise to you. I should have said something yesterday, but I was just so, so scared.'

'That's fair enough.'

She draws in a loud, ragged, sob-strangling breath and looks fearfully at me.

'Stan Fortune is my half-brother. We had the same Mum, we …' The thought of it chokes her up. We wait. She composes herself.

'Sorry … We were quite close when we were little. But we drifted apart, he'd be six, seven years older than me. Then he moved to Sydney, ages ago.'

'When, more or less?'

'I couldn't have been more than about twenty-five –'

'So at least twenty years ago.'

She nods.

'Speak for the tape please, Debbie.'

'Yes, sorry, yes, about that long ago. He was a young adult. He didn't come back much to visit.'

'Can you remember if ever he was in some sort of club? Like a sports club?'

'Yes, yes I do, I mean he was. He was quite a good boxer.'

Faye darts a look at me. The sweet science of bruising, the pugilistic art, Pufferfish in ancient pose on a pavement beneath a barber's pole.

'Do you remember the name of the club?'

'No. It was in Moonah. Somewhere near where the China Diner is, I think.'

'Okay. Go on.'

'When our Mum died, this would be ten years ago, I was, it hit me really hard. Stan came down and arranged everything, paid for everything. He even paid for me and Kate to go and have a few days at the Gold Coast, just to get away and be able to remember Mum and get ready to start again. That was so sweet of him –'

'Kate is?'

'My daughter. She's in second year at Deakin Uni.'

'Did your husband go with you to the Gold Coast?'

'No. Colin was working.'

'Colin being your husband. Colin Hart?'

'Yes.'

She rubs her forehead, massages the side of her face, spreading smears of mascara.

We wait.

'Stan is a barman,' she says.

I'd learnt that myself not half an hour ago. Not that Debbie needs to know.

'In Sydney?'

'Yes. Darlinghurst.'

'Can't pay that well.'

'He's always liked gambling on the dogs. That's what he said. That's how he explained the money.'

'Debbie, a forensic team has counted the money that you put in that backpack. It's over sixty-two thousand dollars. That's a lot of cash.'

'I know.' She takes a gulp of tea, using both hands to minimise her shakes. 'He just came down here out of the blue and told me he'd decided

71

to come and live in Tassie again and he had all this cash from gambling and could I look after it until he'd found a place to rent. I know – I mean I knew, you would know, wouldn't you? – that it was dodgy. But he seemed so happy, unconcerned, confident. As if it was no big deal. And when he offered me twenty thousand of it, I just …' She breaks off, slumps back, looks up at the high ceiling. She starts crying again. Tears run down her cheeks, her neck. She groans. We wait. And when she continues, she's telling it to that fly-specked old ceiling that has gazed dispassionately down on so much grief, rage, remorse.

'I've been having an affair with a man for years. My husband knows. Just not who it is. Colin sleeps with women, I know that, couldn't care less. We stay together for Kate. Funny, habit has kept Colin and me from going through the split. He earns twice as much as me, so he's got that leverage. Unlike Brendan –'

'Brendan is the man you're having the affair with?'

'Yes. He doesn't … unlike someone like Colin, he's got no real job security. Bren's a landscape gardener. He's so good at it, but … so twenty thousand dollars from nowhere would have, it would have set us up so nicely!'

More tears. More tea.

'Did you tell Brendan about the money?'

She shakes her head. I point at the tape.

'No.'

'Why not?'

'I wanted to see that money in my bank, and everything safe. Then it would have been just so nice to surprise him, because he suffers, you know, he's almost my age and we just want to live together. I would have said we should go to the coast near Geelong, he's a mad Cats fan, and we'd be that close to Kate …'

She loses it again. I may be a hard bastard, but I'm not a sadist and I gesture Faye to suspend the interview, which she does, then she helps Debbie up, gives her a little hug and assists her out of the room. They'll go and sit somewhere relatively private and Faye will comfort her and then prompt her to call someone. The husband or the lover, presumably. And a lawyer will help. On the face of it I don't disbelieve Debbie Hart. The pity is that she didn't tell the boyfriend, because now there's no one to corroborate her story of why she agreed to look after Stan's loot. Furthermore, until recently she was hiding sixty-two thousand dollars that had been in the possession of a man brutally murdered. What must I make of that, eh?

72

THERE'S A LOT OF WORK ASSESSING THE FLOOD OF INFORMATION IN response to the new ID, and Hunt wants a comprehensive update of the case at 6 pm today. I know what that means. He'd very much like positive news. If so, there's a reward, otherwise, as I'm aware from long experience, such sessions are bleak. Stan Fortune, it seems, was well known about the traps up there in beautiful, sleazy Sydney. I pop down a level, to Hedda's office. She's not there, but evidence suggests she's not far away, including the scent of a freshly consumed orange and her computer's screensaver not yet operational. Life being what it is, she appears in the door of her office just as I'm looking at the screen.

'Well well,' she says, 'how much are they paying you?'

'Not enough. You can come in, if you like.'

'Ta.' She's holding two apricots in one hand, lobs one at me. 'Canteen special, mate. Fruit's the only thing they can't stuff up. Wolf it down, spiky one, it's good for you.' She bites healthily at hers.

'Wasn't the orange enough?'

Hedda smiles, brushes past me, sits in her chair, uses her long legs to push herself backwards in it, the wheels skittering across the parqet. 'So what can I do for you, snoopy?'

I sit in the plastic orange easy chair alongside the grey filing cabinet, toss the apricot back to her. 'The dead bloke is one Stan Fortune. An identity of sorts on his patch, which was inner and western Sydney. Part wheeler-dealer, part clown. But, they keep referring to his love of bikes.'

'Who's "they"?'

'Public response. And it got me thinking about what you said at the shack about those OMCG wars.'

'He belongs to a gang?'

'Not sure yet.'

'Well let's look.' She propels herself forward and hits computer keys, rapidly calling up AFSSPN, the Australian Federal and State Shared Police Network database.

'What's the prick's name again?'

'Stan Fortune.'

She looks, shakes her head. 'Not here. I heard that he stashed a whole lot of money in the Dynnyrne Child Care Centre. If its bikie-gang related its drugs related, that's for sure.'

'Where did you hear that?'

'Mate, grow up. Canteen goss.'

'Where the rumours are as dodgy as the food. But this one's true, he did. Not sure where the loot came from, though.'

'Mhm … Tell you what Franz, me being proudly childless, kiddy centres give me the creeps, all those unstable little isotopes tearing around crashing into each other. So what's your next move?'

'Sydney.'

'Today?'

I shake my head. 'Hunt pow-wow this evening. There's a bit going on.'

'If it's drugs, that will bring me in.'

'It will.'

IT'S DARK BY THE TIME WE'VE ASSEMBLED FOR THE HUNT BRIEFING. Since there are five of us, we sit at the large Tasmanian-crafted celery top pine, glass and steel table in the conference room annexed to his office. His PA, Priscilla, has garnished the proceedings with a jug of water and glasses. That would have been on his say-so, because this is going to be a discussion, not a meeting. And, not being a big-noter, Hunt parks himself not at a head of the table but halfway down one of its six-chaired sides. Walter, seeking some kind of hierarchical meaning – which Hunt obviously wanted to avoid by sitting where he did – sits opposite him. I choose the corner chair furthest into the room. Rafe and Faye are last in, just, Rafe bagging the corner seat diagonally opposite me and leaving young Faye standing, like this is a game and she's the sucker in the hot seat. She has ten chairs from which to choose. It's a man's world in this place, but Rafe's her kind mentor. Of sorts. He leans a bit and swings the arm of the chair at the head of the table her way, saying, 'All yours, Detective Constable. Sorry. Madam Chair.'

Grif Hunt laughs. So, therefore, does Walter. Faye, excruciatingly conscious of being in this out-of-hours inner male circle, sits and emits a peal of her own female 23-y-o laughter, tapping an imaginary gavel.

Walter reports on Stan Fortune.

'What we know to this point is that he was born in Warrane, went to the primary school there, then Rose Bay High where he dropped out aged fifteen to become an apprentice mechanic. He lived in Warrane with his mother and his half-sister, Debbie, until about age eighteen. No clear picture after that, except for this boxing club link that Franz will tell us about. In Sydney he seems to have only ever been a barman, working at any number of hotels and pubs. No Centrelink record, which is interesting, because you'd guarantee his kind would feed off the dole from time to time.'

'You would,' Hunt says. 'Any indication why not?'

74

'He has a minimal presence, Grif. But for his driver's licence and Medicare card he might as well not exist. Like an outlaw.'

'Yes, the unlikely but not all that unlikely bikie connection.' Hunt employs two pincering fingertips to double-up his generous lower lip. Then he feels his stubble. 'More worrying is that that profile also potentially places him in the never-never where cop meets crim. Faye,' he says, turning to her, 'You'll know from your training that what I'm suggesting is off the record, because talk of police corruption is always awkward and dangerous.'

'Yes, sir.'

'What else Walter?'

'Our Darlinghurst colleagues have done a walk-through of his home, nothing incriminating on the surface. He seems to be a cleanskin. But let's hope they haven't muddied the waters for you, Franz.'

'There should be no reason for it.'

Who knows? We sit in silence and think about it. Then Hunt says, 'Tell us more about him in Tassie, Franz.'

'He told his half-sister that he was planning to come back here to live, and he told the barber who cut his hair that he wanted his old club mates to recognise him. Together they do suggest him wanting to make a new start here. Given that we have an interest in both Debbie Hart and Athol Burden, there may seem little point at this stage in trying to find out who those old club mates are, but I'm not so sure we should ignore it.'

'How can we trust the memory of a young barber traumatised by his mother's death?'

'We can Walter. Paolo Manzini was reasonably sure that that's what Fortune said. The valid point is, why did he want to get in contact with them? Just to renew old ties? There was a boxing club near Gormanston Road called Moonah and Glenorchy Gloves. It burnt down less than a year before Stan left Tasmania. It went by the acronym MAGG. I've been back to the file of the deceased. The tattoo marks on the knuckles of the fists now look enticingly like "MAGG". So I think it's worth pursuing, and Rafe and Faye can get on with that while I'm in Sydney.'

'Good. You know, Faye,' Hunt says, enjoying the chance to impart the wisdom of the venerable to such a raw rookie, 'What sets major crime apart is that the ripples expand so much further across the pool. We've slogged through cases where hundreds of individuals have been interviewed, some repeatedly, from your red-hot suspect through your unreliable eyewitness through to the grandmother of the friend who thought she heard blah blah blah. But it's far better to be thorough from the off.'

'I reckon,' she says.

'And what about your interviewees, Franz?'

'Walter and I agreed not to contest her lawyer's request that Debbie Hart be released on bail. She clearly isn't physically capable of having killed him, and we've no evidence that she contracted others to do it. And although she has a motive, the cash, the psychological profile to do it is just not there. We're also mindful that Athol Burden sits in the frame, and we just have to wait until we have the results of his DNA tests.'

'That's reasonable. Sydney, then?'

'Yes. I'll be on tomorrow's red-eye. I'll be going through his home first off, then I'll get onto his workplaces, his employers and whatever friends or associates come to light. And the ex girlfriend in Townsville. And I also want to talk to someone about the mysterious mobile phone.'

'Good luck!' Rafe laughs. 'I got absolutely nowhere with it. That phone's clean as a showroom car.'

'Which says something. We just don't know what! Okay.' Hunt rises, ambles across to the built-in wall cupboards. 'We at least have a fair degree of forward movement now. I like that. Walter, perhaps a media release tomorrow, that we're investigating a number of new leads, etcetera. Fuzzy but reassuring.'

Hunt brings out his reward. A small sassafras tray, on which are six shot glasses and a bottle of sherry. Not just any old sherry. This is Gutierrez-Colosia Moscatel. Sherry might seem a daggy, unfashionable drink for the big boss to lay on his troops, but up here in his lair, with ice-black winter just through the glass, one of these down the hatch is both warming and, yes, rewarding. It's a Hunt trademark. And we *are* getting somewhere. Slowly – but somewhere.

The fiery river of sherry sends us optimistically out and into the bitter cold.

9

BIG NEWS — HOBART INTERNATIONAL AIRPORT HAS A PROPER BAGGAGE carousel. No longer will we stand about in the elements searching for luggage piled on the back of an airport trailer. I'll look forward to that when I get back. For now I'm content to stand around, just another traveller, overcoat across one arm, briefcase hanging from the paw of the other.

Time and the traveller have a strange relationship. I'm suddenly looking down twenty-five thousand feet at two big dents in Tassie's northern coastline east of the Tamar mouth. Noland Bay and Anderson Bay they'd be.

Another time-flip, another aircraft, a much bigger Airbus now, and a captain revising his Sydney forecast to 'thunderstorm activity' and suggesting that 'for our comfort' we buckle up now. Charming. The plane whinges and whines in descent, dropping alarmingly through driving rain uncomfortably close to the roofs of suburbs.

I sit in the back of taxis for a good reason. Having an occupation which involves a great deal of talking to strangers in intimate spaces, I don't want to indulge in the same when that can be avoided. My luck, then, to get stuck with a motormouth, a Jordanian who wants to be a property developer, who mistrusts governments and their hidden agendas, and who has never been to Tasmania because it's too cold and full of devils and why do we call them that and aren't they all dead anyway because they bit each other and got cancer or something?

Close, unseasonable heat, chaotic noise and a cocktail of smells greet me outside the Kirketon Hotel in Darlinghurst, where I've booked for one night. But it's lunchtime and I'm bloody hungry. In Taylor Square there's a promising looking burger place and it's right next to the copshop.

The foyer of the hotel is clogged with a package tour of exhausted-looking Koreans. Large suitcases are neatly lined up in bulging rows. A fresh-faced concierge in a smart black suit seems to have the universe under his personal control. I check in and elevate to my room, where I've a glorious fifteenth-floor view of two blocks of flats.

I cross the now-empty foyer, step into the heat. I'm walking towards a woman and she's watching me. She's about fifty and she looks intelligent, well-educated. But the bulging faded green recycling bags, her life's possessions, tell the story. I deviate slightly to avoid walking into her.

'Can I have five dollars please?'

She looks tired. Worn out. On I go.

'Hey, it's to feed my kid. Come on.'

I look her in the eye and shake my head marginally.

'Two dollars.' She stinks. Her shoes are cracked.

'Fuck off then!' she says loudly to my back. And is obviously watching me walking to the station, because behind my back, in my shit-brown coat, she turns up the volume: '*You stingy fucking cop! Go and fuck yourself you cunt!*' Sydneysiders have heard it all before; they're barely aware of me entering the station. I give my details to the duty officer. I'm expected. She makes a call.

The last time I did business with Wally Quarry he was very much my junior, but now he's like me, a major crime DI, homicide in his case. He's still young but he's shot up the ranks. My guess is that he's a bristle of the new broom trying to sweep clean. I've witnessed the same in Tassie. Magnus took a big fall when the old guard was targeted for removal, rightly or wrongly suspected of being corrupt. Magnus's case was tough. He wasn't bent, but nor was he entirely straight. Just like nature, where there is no such thing as straight. Here in Sydney, though, there are real problems, deep-rooted problems. So I'm told, and I trust my source, DS Hedda Andover.

Wally Quarry bounces out of the lift, all energy. Large thin ears, a cropped nut, spiky ginger tash, bomber jacket, faded blue jeans. In this part of the sporting world he'd be a scrum half, maybe a hooker. What he doesn't look like is a newly minted senior cop, which is perfectly understandable, given my recent contretemps with the bag lady.

'Mate, good to see you again, how are we?' Quarry gives me a handshake as generous as his smile. 'Tassie's baddest keeping you on your toes I trust!'

'Too quiet there, Wally, so I sent myself here.'

He mock groans. 'We could do with an extra hand or three.' He stabs the lift's summons button with an ironman forefinger. 'Hardly anything on your dead fella, to be honest.'

'Anything is something. This time last week he was a skinhead called Tom Jones.'

'True enough, always pays to look on the bright side.' He ushers me into the lift.

Once we're seated in his glassed-off DI workspace in a large, sparsely populated open plan area he's all business – suddenly a man pressed for time. I'm a cop from a remote region with a body that's no apparent problem of his.

'Here's what we were able to put together.'

He slides a thin manila folder across the desk. They're always manila and they're usually thin. 'A pretty basic life history, Franz. Stan Fortune's a cleanskin as far as our records go. There are a coupla connections might give you something. The employer. And there's an ex. Your Stan seems to be one of those blokes who's managed to offend no one, works in a pub, tinkers with his bike, end of life story. So either he is that or he's managed to minimise his existence, *for purposes unknown.*'

It's a strange emphasis, as if he's parodying himself playing a cop in a bad TV movie. But I know what he means. Why bash and execute a nonentity far from his home? I open the folder. Quarry's up again, boundless energy, wants to be somewhere else. But there's me.

'Tea, coffee, mate?'

'A tea would be good. Brown, no sugar.'

He darts from his glass box and I flick through the meagre contents of the folder. This routine police file's not why I've flown a thousand kilometres into a thunderstorm. The Stan Fortune they've prepared for me is a cardboard cut-out of the Stan Fortune who not only never troubled them, but whose life history you could spread on a Sao biscuit. Driver's licence, bank records – no suspicious transactions – landline and mobile phone records – all certified as clean – a patchy employment record in the hospitality industry listing half a dozen licensed premises going back nearly twenty years. There are names and contact details of a handful of known associates. Home computer checked as clean. And a few photos of him, the file note advising that they were removed from his home for the purposes of compiling this 'dossier'. Some dossier.

One photo's of our late nobody in best penguin garb shaking up a cocktail. Probably a promo for wherever he was working at the time. Another's with a girlfriend. In another he's posing in full leathers alongside a Kawasaki 900 cc, helmet under one bowed arm, grinning.

New machine by the look of it, proud owner. The pics aren't recent. No doubt he took to mobile phone technology to record his more recent life – the mobile his killers probably chucked away, along with his driver's license, wallet, and whatever else nailed him as Stan Fortune. Except for those keys around his neck. And the question still buzzing lazily around Pufferfish's head, like a housefly around a light bulb hanging from a ceiling, is why visit extreme foul play upon someone who swam between the flags?

Quarry returns with my tea and a colleague. Quaint old bastard that I am, I rise smartly.

'Franz, this is Chief Super Gillian Yinakis. Heads up our Drug Squad.'

We shake hands. She's short, slim, dark-featured, late-forties tops.

'Hello, Franz. Welcome to our patch.'

And unusually soft-spoken.

'Good to meet you, Gillian. As you can see, Wally's being the perfect host.' I wave at my Yarra River tea. It's in a too-large cup in too-small saucer, which Wally managed to slop against the edge of the manila folder, not that he appears to have noticed. She, I think, wonders if I'm being sarcastic. She emits a mild chuckle.

'Service is our motto, Franz.'

'Congratulations on your appointment, Gillian.'

'Our news travels that far, does it, and so quickly?'

'Hedda told me.'

'Of course! How is she?'

Quarry's eyeballing us like he's watching a game of ping-pong.

'Well, I believe. Enjoying the change from big to not-that-small island.'

What Gillian doesn't know is that I know she was one of Hedda's referees when Hedda applied to transfer to Tasmania.

'Give her my best regards.'

I nod, struck by the remarkable physical stillness of her and the unblinking, slightly hypnotic gaze emanating from her large dark eyes. She has about her the air of a frequent visitor to the other side, not a hot-seat corruption-busting drug cop. But then she probably could do with a slice of the paranormal, having to simultaneously wage war on international drug lords and her own errant troops, who probably also resent a sheila barking, or in her case whispering, orders at them.

'I thought I'd drop by because Stan Fortune's been mentioned in dispatches, Franz.'

'Really?' I glance at Quarry. He's said nothing about this. He says, 'You know how it goes, mate. Gill and I were having yak in the canteen yesterday and I mentioned your visit ...'

'Now I've got that Tasmanian link through Hedda,' she adds, 'my ears always prick up. And when Wally mentioned the name Stan Fortune, it rang a bell. You'll know how deep we're in the bikie warfare.'

'Yes. The Revs, Drags and the raided drug warehouse.'

'Wall-to-wall, coming out of our bloody ears. Three dead from that incident, and the body count's now seven, with that number again seriously injured. And it's far from over. My task force has interviewed any number of people, gang members, girfriends, family members, witnesses, and one name among the hundreds entered in the investigation database is Stan Fortune's.'

'What circumstances?'

'The officer who entered it had interviewed an ex-bikie who said he thought Stan Fortune might belong to a club.'

'One of the warring clubs?'

She looks doubtful, a bit regretful. 'The record of interview doesn't say that. And as you can see from this' – she gestures at the manila folder – 'there really isn't anything else we're aware of linking him to either gang, or any other gang for that matter. So, considering we know of nearly 700 active bikie gang members across New South Wales, your fellow's pretty much off the radar. Except that he was murdered.'

'Which is why we thought we'd run it by you, mate.' Quarry says.

'You might uncover something more while you're here,' she adds. Unlike her mild voice, her gaze seems to insist upon it.

'I might.' I turn my attention back to Quarry. 'Those details I sent through to you of the mobile phone we found wrapped in a sock in his suitcase. Has Gillian's unit run them through their records?'

'One big central database here, mate. It's called information sharing. That phone was purchased in a false name and the number stored in it's untraceable.'

She's interested. 'Let me have a look at the details, anyway. That's a level of criminal sophistication in a local barman I'd like to know more about.'

Gillian Yinakis hands me her card. I return the favour.

'Good-o,' Quarry says, evidently pleased to have matched us up. 'Well, Franz, get outside your cuppa, mate and we'll shoot round to Fortune's place.'

Gillian shakes my hand again. 'Good to meet you. Do you see much of Hedda, by the way?'

'We bump into each other occasionally.'

She leaves the glass box. I'm impressed. Much more impressed than I am with the taste of her colleague's so-called tea.

In the lift on the way down a big lumbering bloke gets in. Big as in 200 cm, six-six in the old days, and a solid 100 kg. Where Quarry is a nifty scrum half this man is all cauliflower ears and engine room grunt, able to compress a scrum of opposition meat into steaming green turf. He's got greying, wavy hair thick enough to surf off, like an old style Yugoslav bad guy.

Quarry intros. 'Franz, Detective Hugh Hughes, Hugh this is DI Franz Heineken, Tasmania.'

We shake hands, in that my hand is monstered in his. His expression is not cold but not warm. I would describe it as luke-dead.

'Hugh is one of Gillian's', Quarry says. Hughes rolls his eyes at the mention of her name, as if I should know all about why. Well, I don't. He's dressed as an old-fashioned cop, tasteless trousers, thin collar, wide '70s tie and factory-issue slip-on shoes. I wouldn't buy a used car from him.

'How's Tassie?' His voice is a bass rumble.

'Wet, cold and miserable.'

'Franz is on the dead body case,' Quarry says.

'Rum business,' Hugh Hughes mumbles, as the lift bumps to a halt and his bulk vanishes through the sliding doors.

IT'S A REASONABLY QUICK TRIP IN QUARRY'S UNMARKED COMMODORE from Taylor Square to a cul-de-sac near Kippax Street and a small, detached red brick house on a standard block. Fortune's humble home has a driveway, garage, there's a spiky lawn full of bald patches, one miserable-looking scrawny tree, a letterbox overflowing with damp junk mail. Along the boarded-up windows and door a long strip of NSW Police crime scene tape is intact.

'Best we could do,' Quarry says, unlatching the bent little gate. 'Plus we have night patrols come by.'

He unlocks the front door and we duck under the crime scene tape. He puts on lights. 'Want me to stick around?'

'No need. I'll give you a call when I'm through.'

'Catch you later then.' He hands me a bunch of keys and ducks back out and I take my first focused look at the place. There's no mistaking the occupant's lifestyle. In one corner of the lounge-room stands the shrine, an obscenely large plasma TV screen. Facing it is a large stained leather armchair with more levers and buttons than a flight deck. Alongside the chair, a low occasional table. On it, and on the carpet around the chair, empty fast-food packets and containers, crushed beer cans, messy tabloid newspapers, glossy Aussie sports mags. His DVD collection is, was, big, and typical, movies, games, porn. Not a Simon Schama in sight. There's also a music system. The landline phone's on the floor in one corner. I push the message button: 'Message one, this message was stored too long and has been erased. Message two, this message was stored too long and has been erased. Message three, this message was stored too long and has been erased.'

His bedroom's just as crappy, though the king-sized bed and standing robes would together have been a good fifteen grand, add another ten for the carpet and double that all again for the en suite bathroom. Unkempt, unwashed clothes in forgotten piles, a ceiling mirror, a smaller but still big TV. The robes are jammed with sharp-man clothes, some of them look as if they've never been worn. Boxes of motorbike parts litter the second bedroom, a workshop of sorts. Crappy kitchen, crappier bathroom and toilet, and a back yard of uneven, cracked, moss-lined red bricks, the moss fed by a dripping tap. I see, but don't acknowledge, a neighbour over the high, lantana-weighted mutual fence, a middle-aged bloke whose hairy face vanishes behind a lace curtain. I'll talk to him soon enough.

The locked and bolted garage tells me something. No motorbike. One jet ski in good condition on its trailer, but no bike. Where is it? The Kawasaki registered in his name was never aboard the *Spirit of Tasmania* ferry. Perhaps he had it in the mystery Mitsubishi van, the key to which was around his neck. A finger-wipe of the inside of the exhaust pipes, and the film of salt on the duco, tell me he used the jet ski not long before he left for Tassie. Here's that near-comatose bloody fly around my head again. What I have here is information, but it's without meaning. I need a human. When I cut my constabulary teeth – decades ago – a wise old Rotterdam homicide cop with baggy eyes said to me, Franz, if you want to be a successful cop, ask questions. Ask, ask, ask until you are sick of asking, and then ask once more, and that once more might just give the answer you need.

The peeping neighbour doesn't take long to open the door to his place, perhaps because I've knocked with a loud cop directness.

'What can I do for ya, mate?' A beefy, gravel-voiced man, barefoot, fat-legged in cheap grey trackies, torso spilling unpleasantly from every available gap in a Big W check shirt with half its buttons gone. Built like a shit housebrick, as Rafe would say. His browny-grey facial whiskers extend hugely down his rugby league neck onto his chest, disappear under the black-green shirt and re-emerge in wiry profusion on the forearms, one of which bears a tattoo of a snake-encoiled busty woman with come-on eyes. He ought to have firebreaks shaved on him. And he smells.

I flick my ID at him. 'I'd like to ask you some questions about your neighbour.'

'You blokes already did.'

'Ever seen me before?'

'Jeez, keep your hair on, mate.'

'You could teach me about that. Did you socialise with him? Speak much?'

'Just neighbours, but yeh, a how-are-ya.'

'First name terms?'

He nods. 'It was, "How are ya Stan, good thanks Bluey." Mate, I know he was knocked off, down in Twoheadmainya of all places, but don't look at me for why. Bloke had that bike of his, had a girl, liked his beer, forever walkin' in with a slab. Loud music, but who gives a shit these days about that.'

'That it?'

'Yeah, that's bloody it!'

'You were having a good perv at me through your kitchen window, Bluey, so I wonder if you did the same and maybe saw Stan with, you know, some interesting visitors at any time.'

'Nuh.'

'The girlfriend?'

'Came and went, just a chick. Haven't seen her for a while, but.'

'See – that's information, Bluey.'

He gives me a withering look. Dickhead Cop 1, Bluey 0. 'Mate, if Stan Fortune got up to no good, he didn't do it from this house of his.'

Make that one-all.

'What about the jet ski, Bluey?'

'Oh yeah, Stan liked his jet ski. His bike and his jet ski.'

'You'd watch him tow the jet ski away?'

'Yeh, sometimes.'

'What car?'

'*His* car, mate.'

'I don't see it out there.'

This perplexes him briefly, then he says, 'Shit, that's right. He came with a hire van. I saw him get out of it, wondered if he was gunna move house.'

'And?'

'And what?'

'How long ago was this?'

'Jeez. Three weeks?'

'Why do you say it was a hire van?'

''Cause it had the name on it, mate!'

'That name is?'

'Uh … got me there – wait on – PJM. Yep. Port Jackson Movers.'

'Could that van have fitted his motorbike?'

'Easy.'

'You're a fount of information Bluey.'

'No bloody need to put the mockers on, mate.'

'Thanks for your help.'

On my way back to Fortune's I ring Quarry and ask him to send a uniform to the hire place. And a reminder to check those messages stored too long.

STAN FORTUNE'S LAST EMPLOYER ISN'T AS DAGGY AS BLUEY. HE'S WORSE. He's like his Parramatta disco: a sleazy, cop-allergic cash magnet. I talk to him in his aftershave-reeking office above a black-walled expanse of dance floor, bar counter, ceiling strobes, a pole dance stage, and pool and darts zones for the boys between shows. That he's an oily creep with a three-day growth is neither here nor there. I need information, and of the solid kind.

'So what do you want to know, detective?'

'His work hours, and what he was like as a person.'

'Wednesday to Saturday here, four pm 'til late. One of my better barmen. Reliable. Almost head-hunted in the trade.'

' "Almost"?'

'Not quite rolled gold. Reliable, though. You could set your clock by him. I don't employ losers.'

'That's good of you. Why did you rate him so highly?'

'Knew the job. Never lost money. Could control unruly patrons. Friendly. I could leave the place to him if anything came up. Which it did from time to time. The regulars knew Stan well and liked him. He was almost a fixture. But he also had sharp antennae, if you know what I mean. Great listener.'

'That helped you?'

'Stan could head 'em off at the pass, if you get my drift. He could sense if a blue might be coming on, warn me.'

'You must have liked him.'

'As an employee? Yeah. As a bloke? No comment.'

'What do you mean?'

'Behind the penguin front he was a wannabe, a pretender. A barman with stars in his eyes, a dickhead, let's be honest. Stan Fortune was a middle-aged nobody. Dunno if it he'd had ADD or what's it, attention deficit delivery. Fast talker, y'know that rapid delivery? Great asset if you're making a stranger a drink. B-minus otherwise. He was no Paul Hogan crossed with Hugh Jackman. If I can put it that way.'

'So as your employee he had no enemies that you know of?'

'Totally none. In fact he almost knew everyone too well.'

'Meaning?'

'Great bartender! Everyone welcome. Stan could get to know a stranger quick smart. Like an old mate. It's a gift you look for in staff selling alcohol. Stan never didn't know what was going on in his bar. Who was there, with who, the vibe. He could be wiping a schooner dry and looking that way, but his ears'd be tuned the other way, listening, picking it all up. Great listener. As a bar owner you pay good dollar for that. Well, good for this area. The Rocks, he'd be on three grand a week.'

'So in that sense he was on top of things.'

'Mate, yeah, but it was coming to an end.'

'What do you mean?'

'I'm planning to move fully into girls. That means ramped up security. And the firm I've been negotiating with provide all staff. That meant no Stan.'

'And you told him that?'

'Yeah.'

'A bikie gang security firm?'

'Could be. That's my business.'

'Members of the Revs?'

'Hey, what's this? Who I employ is my business! It's all legit.'

My mobile rings. Walter. The fool must want an update. Wouldn't I call him if I had something to report? He can wait. Then again, Stan's most recent employer has given me what I need, a picture. Harmless stickybeak no-enemies Stan, about to lose his job. Is that so, eh?

'WALTER? FRANZ.' I'M ON THE PAVEMENT OUTSIDE THE BAR, SCOWLING at the afternoon sun and noise.

'You might as well come back, Franz, we've got our man. Athol Burden's blood test is positive. His blood is on the deceased's clothes.'

'What does Hunt say?'

'That it's difficult to argue against a positive blood sample on a murdered man. We'd be derelict if we didn't act on this. The onus is now on Burden to explain himself, but this time he can do it from remand.'

The noise, traffic, voices, music, means I'm pushing the mobile against my ear, taking in this development while trying to avoid oncoming pedestrians. There's something unreal about it. I'd like Rafe's opinion, seeing he and I did the first Burden interview, but in my absence it's Walter's call. He'll want Burden in a van ASAP and I can see why.

'You there Franz?'

'Sorry, noise.' I break from the human flow into a barred piss-reeking doorway. 'Okay, you'd better bring him in, then. Nothing much to report here. But there's a few more of his associates I want to talk to.'

'Any point in that now?'

'Yes, because I'm here.'

'Suit yourself.'

I look for a taxi. They're all over the place, all full. There's a small park about a block away. A walk in it will be good. A walk and a long, hard think. I'm just ever so slightly concerned that Athol isn't, in fact, our man. The more I don't learn about Stan, the more I'm inclined to place him in company decidedly more villainous than Athol Burden. Stan must have absorbed a great deal of information while working in his sleazy bars, and what is information if it isn't valuable to someone?

Good old Wally. He sent a uniform to Port Jackson Movers and, yes, they obediently produced a car, parked in their lot since its owner, Tom Jones, hired a Mitsubishi van and they haven't seen him since.

All in all, my trip to Sinney hasn't been entirely in vain. And I wonder, maybe I hope, that I haven't heard the last of Gillian Yinakis, well in the top fifty most powerful individuals in New South Wales, and with her spooky interest in my case.

THE SYDNEY-BRISBANE FLIGHT IS A BIT UP AND DOWN BUT OTHERWISE straightforward. The Boeing 767 executes an extended bank to port over North Stradbroke Island and straightens a few ks behind a Qantas jumbo which came in over the Pacific. Touchdown's good. Time for a coffee and a glance at the *Courier-Mail* before I'm up again, this time in a brand new 737 which climbs rapidly to its 10,000 metres and cruising speed of 625 kph. I'll be in this one for just under two hours, arriving in Townsville at midday. My in-flight neighbour, a tanned, leather-skinned cockie, insists on being, well, neighbourly, introducing himself as Phil and shaking my hand.

'Where ya from, cob?' Phil asks, while wrestling with his seat belt.

'Hobart.'

'Onya. Holidayin' in Townsville?'

'No, business.'

'You'll like the place, anyway. Pity you can't get in a few days R&R, she's made for it. You know what gets my goat? People slag off Townsville because she's an industrial port. A dump, they reckon, only dependent on her harbour. Well, I'm here to tell you that's crap. But people put the boot into Hobart too, don't they cob?'

'They do. Too cold, too remote, too small.'

'Jealous bastards. Jealous of us enjoying a quality lifestyle and none of the hassles you get living in a big, stinking effing place.'

I haven't been able to find out what the ex does in Townsville. Maybe Phil can clue me in.

'What's your main earner these days?'

'Sugar, sugar and sugar. Nah, more than that. All the Ida-Cloncurry stuff, the copper, the zinc and LGM concentrates, your lead, your nickel. And the inland stations. Then of course we import and refine a hell of a tonnage of nickel ore. And we bring in a fair whack of oil and fertilizer and cement. That enough for ya?'

'I'm impressed.'

'Townsville's the centre of the known universe, cob.' He cackles. A steward and her trolley await our pleasure. Phil wants a Bundie and coke. Nothing for me. I open my briefcase and start working. He tries to restart the dialogue. Not happening, Phil. He arcs up, disbelieving then narked, as if we should step outside and settle it like blokes, but then he gets the message, sucks on his juice like a good boy and finds something to look at through his porthole.

When we descend it's through low, dense cloud. I'm reminded of mid-winter fog in the Derwent Valley, damp and stingingly cold. I've never been a heat person, but the wall of it waiting for me outside the aeroplane is oddly reassuring. Perhaps because it's so all-embracing. And now I'm reminded of a late-summer northerly, Tassie-style, threatening a firestorm, except, and it's a big except, this air is heavy with moisture.

Tall palm trees line the apronside façade of the terminal building and inside it, in stark contrast to Sydney, the faces are noticeably Anglo. Bit like Tasmania was until we began welcoming our east African refugees.

The taxi into town takes all of ten minutes. I'm staying in the Travelodge. It's round, tall and sticks out above the place. It even has a nickname, the Sugar Shaker, according to the taxi driver. In the mall outside it groups of Aborigines are sitting about, and the palm trees down the centre of the mall are alive with wildly chirping lorikeets.

Angie Steele presents herself at the Townsville Police Station just after two. I can cope with her being a few minutes late. Had she done a runner that would surely have implicated her in the business. And pissed me off immeasurably. The eloquence of a thousand Phils would not have made the trip worthwhile. She's brought into the interview room in which I'm waiting, the constable closing the door behind us. I stand, motion her to the plastic seat opposite. Strangers across a scarred, stained table. Her face is lined, long dyed black hair, big lipstick, eyeliner, tight white cotton top, tight green jeans, nico-stained fingers.

'Thanks for coming along, Angie. I won't take too much of your time.' I hold out my ID. She leans forward a bit, squints at it, unlikely she can read a word. It's my ugly mug, though, and that seems to be good enough for her as she leans back in the chair, folds her arms.

'What do you want to know, detective?' Smoker's voice.

'I'm sorry about the circumstances of my being here.'

She shrugs. 'We hadn't been hitched for a while.'

'How long?'

'Six, eight months, I reckon.'

'And how long had you been together?'

'Maybe five, six years.'

'You lived at his place?'

'No, I had my own flat. But yeah, I stayed there a lot. And sometimes he stayed at mine. It was that kind of arrangement.'

'Can I ask why you split up?'

'Mutual indifference … mainly mine!' She coughs a crackly laugh from troubled lungs.

'No hard feelings?'

'Stan wouldn't of known a hard feeling if it slapped him in the face.'

'A soft touch?'

She shakes her head. 'No, he had his standards. I saw him threaten to bash a bloke once with a broken bottle. But that was extreme. The coke talking. Mainly Stan was like an old leather armchair, everyone knew him and knew he was soft.'

'Can you think of why anyone would want to kill him?'

'No, mate. Stan didn't make enemies. That was one of the better things about him. Almost too many friends, if you know what I mean.'

'Not exactly.'

'He knew everyone. Everyone knew him. Pick a hidden enemy out of that!'

'Well he annoyed someone, Angie.'

'Yeah, but down in Tassie, right?'

'Did you know he grew up there?'

'Oh yeah, he'd mention the place now and then. If there was something on the news or whatever. Princess Mary. Ricky Ponting. Protestors up trees.'

'Did he ever talk specifically about Tasmania? About old friends, say?'

'Uhm …' She looks about the place, slight frown, hands fiddling. Needs a smoke already. 'Not that I remember, no.'

'What about old friends from a boxing club?'

'Mate, you know what, I could do with a tube.'

'I'll suspend the interview in a minute. Old friends from a boxing club?'

'Shit yeah, now that you mention it.' She holds up her left hand, not to show me that it's shaking and she really could do with firing up that tube, but as a fist, and she taps the digits below the knuckles. 'Stan had tatts here. Letters, you couldn't see what. I remember once asking him and he said he'd been a really good boxer in Tassie. Mate, I thought that was funny, 'cause the Stan Fortune I knew wouldn't of looked too flash running around in a ring in his bathers with some mad bastard after him. But he said he belonged in some kind of special group and that they beat the shit out of all comers.'

'So what made him go all soft, Angie? You're telling me he wasn't much of a he-man. But he must have been reasonably fit. The bike. The jet ski.'

'No, mate. Stan smoked heaps, like me, and he was, y'know, lazy. And a skinny runt. And he wouldn't dare start a punch-up at his age. Patrons he dealt with, they'd knock his scone off.'

I nod, waiting. She wants up and into that fresh air for a hit, drills suddenly avid fingernails on the table.

'Tell me what more you can about this boxing group, Angie. Until you do, we're staying put.'

'There's nothing!'

'Okay. Did Stan ever visit Tasmania?'

90

'Not that I would know, but no. When we were an item, anytime he left Sydney we went together. On hols.'

'Did he get any Tassie visitors?'

'Seriously, mate, no. Honest. The place just didn't feature in his life.'

'Okay, Angie. Interview suspended for the purposes of Ms Steele having a cigarette.' I depress the off button, and out we go. I take her to a small internal courtyard where she can light up.

'Tea, Angie?'

'Got coffee?'

'I'm sure they do. And plenty of sugar, if you want it.'

SEATED AGAIN SHE'S MORE RELAXED, SIPS HER COFFEE IN ITS CHIPPED mug, even manages a hint of a reflective smile. 'Stan was a good bloke, really. Why'd someone want to job him?'

'As I'm sure you know, he arrived in Tasmania under a false name and he had a large sum of money on him. Why do you think he would try to hide his identity?'

'Got me, mate.'

'He was "Tom Jones"? Does that mean anything?'

'Nah. How much money?'

'Enough to be a worry. The proceeds of a crime, most likely. Did he work in cash at all?'

'Funny you should say that. Jeez mate, you know how to press the buttons! He used to treat me to things, right? He'd be like, "I've got some dough, do you want a fur coat", or, "let's go to Bali for a few days".'

'How often did this happen?'

'Two or three times a year, maybe.'

'And you asked where he got it from?'

'Not, really, no. I reckoned, y'know, some business at the pub. Luck at the pokies.'

'Come on Angie, I wasn't born yesterday.'

'Oh mate, selling tabs or something? The pubs he worked in were those kinds of places.'

'Would you have any evidence, other than sums of cash, for him selling drugs?'

'Couple of his mates were a bit suss.'

'Regular mates?'

'Yeah ... you could say so. Or maybe not! Everyone knew Stan the barman, and he knew everyone.'

91

'So who exactly were these mates?'

'Stan was a mad keen biker. He spent years and years trying to get into this or that club, but he could never get a member to sponsor him. They were always like, "take a concrete pill, Stan – harden up!" He was a skinny little boxer gone to seed.' She laughs, somehow manages to stifle her smoker's hack.

'Which gangs?'

'Like, the Revs. He was always on the fringes, never good enough.'

'Never bad enough, Angie.'

'Yeah!'

'Did he bring any of these characters home? Did you socialise with them?'

'No mate, never. I reckon he had a rule about that to himself. All the friends were mine – the eating out, the days on the jet skis, the parties. About the only weird thing was one day I was walking to his place and he was sitting in some bloke's car. This is not so long ago. They were talking and Stan didn't like that I, you know, sprung them.'

'What kind of bloke?'

'Big. A big bulky bloke with thick grey … you know that kind of hair that's wavy? And a sort of heavy face, if you know what I mean. Collar and tie. I thought, that's unusual.'

'You've got a good memory, Angie.'

'Well I did peer in, mate! Just to check that Stan was okay.'

'Good on you. So how did he explain it?'

'He didn't. Just said later, something to do with work …'

Good timing being what it is, she erupts in a coughing fit just as my mobile beeps a message received. She starts waving an apologetic hand, the other gripping the table, and I'm up, moving smartly out of phlegm flack range and reading the message from Rafe: *hey boss athol burden tried to do a runner we picked him up at the ferry might as well come home mate.*

10

I SNATCH MY OVERNIGHT BAG OFF THE REVOLVING CAROUSEL OF THE arrivals hall of Hobart International Airport, find my car, shed the trusty faecal-brown coat, shoot through, listening to ABC Radio's AM program, the voice leading off with a grim story of Pakistanis marching in thousands to preserve the rule of law in that land of complexity. Sheet rain falls across the Organ Pipes of Mount Wellington and the dark-green silhouette of hills linking it to Mount Dromedary. Sunlight slants through shifting cloud masses. From the eastern shore, approaching the bridge, Hobart and her suburbs, and the pair of flags rippling energetically at Government House, have a strange unreality about them, a hyper-reality brought on by a massive rainbow. This place is home to the likes of me. And who am I? Just a cop. A man whose identity is well known to himself but who, sifting after and hunting down the rotten elements, the breakers of civilisation's codes, assumes himself to have a higher status. Really? Says who? I never knew Stan Fortune. I met him for the first time in a deer bag buried badly under beach sand, his greeting an appalling stench. Then I, we, put bits and pieces together. And now, apparently, we have his killer, with more seemingly damaging evidence against him having come to light while I was interstate.

Walter stands. In Hunt's lair, he has the full attention of his audience. The gravitas of the occasion imbues him with a visible energy, his steps light, his eyes bouncing off us. He even shoots a cuff. Talk about showing off. But what he's about to say is important. Still, he's showing off, which is to say, I'll forever reserve the right to dislike him and give him credit for as little as I can. He's an efficient public face though, I do grant him that, and he's had the public in the palm of his hand for years, since the day he by dint of luck successfully negotiated a tricky hostage situation involving a deranged de facto and her terrified young stepson.

He's at the large whiteboard, which he's clearly spent a long time crowding with his neat but sloping blue writing, each paragraph having its own empty little rectangle alongside. He undoes the button of his jacket in order to allow his arm the flexibility to wield the blue marker.

'The case against Athol Burden is overwhelming,' Walter says. 'We have so many ticked boxes that a jury can only find him guilty beyond reasonable doubt. So let's start ticking, troops. Tick one, Burden and Fortune stayed at the same time in the Alexander Pearce Hotel, known for its hospitality to elements of the criminal class. Apparent strangers to one another, they drank rowdily together. Tick two, on or about the day Fortune was murdered Burden departed the APH, even though he still had four paid nights available to him there. The reason he gave for leaving early, embarrassment and annoyance through a sexual arrangement with a prostitute gone wrong, cannot be proved by him. Tick three, the body of murdered Fortune was found in a deer bag, of a type used by Burden in the course of his profession, that is, as a shooter of feral and wildlife pests. Tick four, the handgun used to murder Fortune hasn't been found, but the calibre is of a type of gun once owned by Burden but which he has mysteriously lost. Tick five, Burden is of a physical capability to have carried Fortune to his beach grave and buried him.

'Tick six, Burden lied to us when he said he has never left Tasmania in his life, when in fact he stayed in a Kings Cross hotel in Sydney shortly before Fortune came to Tasmania, a hotel not far from Fortune's home. Explaining that he lied to us because he hadn't told his wife, because he didn't want her to know, she thinking he was on the other side of the Western Tiers looking for fox scats, just won't wash in court. He's not on the Fox Taskforce, for one. And tick seven, Burden as we now have learnt has a compelling motive, in that he owes the Australian Taxation Office some forty thousand dollars and that debt, passed onto a debt collection agency, has him imminently faced with repossession of his property and a possible jail term.

'And finally tick eight, his blood is on the clothing of the murdered man. Burden's explanation, that he took aspirins to thin his blood to reduce his blood pressure, a side effect being the aspirins causing nosebleeds, one of which must have happened during their brief struggle, also cannot be proved by him. Furthermore he has no doctor's record recommending that treatment, and because the GP who he said suggested the remedy is a Mozambican national who was in Tasmania on a visa and who subsequently moved to the island of Madagascar to practise, that island now under lockdown due to a military coup, means that that doctor is impossible to contact, if indeed he ever made the spurious aspirin suggestion. All that we have to consider is how and why the money Fortune brought with him was associated with Burden, or why he told Burden about it.'

'It's overwhelmingly neat, Walter,' I say. 'And that's why it troubles me. Look, for our part we can't prove that Burden went to Sydney to meet Fortune. We can't prove that Burden knew that Fortune had a stash of money hidden in a Hobart child care centre. Yes, Burden has his compelling motive, money, but that doesn't translate into murder, because we don't have hard evidence that he did the deed. We can't disprove that his nose bled onto Fortune's jeans. We need the murder weapon. And I have others to interview.'

'Franz, let a jury decide. We have a body, now we have a prime suspect. What if the gun had been found with the body, unregistered and wiped clean of prints? Would we then be saying, oh well, bad luck us, you can go home now Athol? No. We have a sufficiently strong case. Burden's innocent until proved guilty, but in this case he's surely going to have to prove that he's not guilty, because the odds are stacked that high against him.'

Hunt intercedes. Clearly, his silence has been indicative of how tricky this is. We're cops, not lottery specialists. If we put this up and it goes to trial and gets turfed out, a judge bad-mouthing us for an inept case and picking on an innocent rural Taswegian, the image of the force will take a hit. On the other hand, if we don't press charges, for lack of that final nail in the coffin, we'll be roasted for allowing a 'killer' to roam free. It's happened before here, with high profile unsolved murders continuing to stir much feeling, as they're raised again and again in the media. What's the answer? Walter wants the prosecution, wants the media fed that way. Me, no. The job of the media is to report, not to galvanise, they're journalists, not roofmakers.

'You have a difficulty, Franz. You're relying on relationships that ended twenty years ago or more.'

'That's true. But they are legitimate lines of inquiry. I need to eliminate them from the investigation. And to avoid giving a free kick to a defence counsel, that we didn't investigate every possible avenue. And there's information to come through from Sydney relating to phone calls. Let's see what that is. And the media release on the Port Jackson Movers van might bring something.'

'Alright, alright. You had better get moving then.'

'On my way.'

Walter doesn't like it. But he holds his tongue. I can see by his expression what he's thinking. If I hold up the case against the real killer while I'm on my goose chase, that won't do me any good in the wash-up.

Prick.

11

SO HERE WE GO WITH A LINE OF INQUIRY THAT'S NOT, IN FACT,
supposed to go anywhere. Stubborn old Dutch bastard that I am,
I look forward to the dead end. In the meantime how do you get to
Triabunna from Hobart? You drive east away from the mountain past
the so-called international airport, Barilla Bay oyster farm and the golf
clubs, then cross the causeways into Sorell township where, faced with
the stark choice to turn left or right, you choose the former. Proceed
for a while – taking in Black Charlie's Opening and Bust-Me-Gall Hill –
and, notwithstanding a torturously narrow road along the Prosser River,
you're suddenly at Orford, summer haunt of the public service, and the
turquoise waters of the east coast. Triabunna is nearby, its backdrop the
spectacular mountains of uninhabited Maria Island. The township has
its own peaks, pyramids in fact, composed of woodchips, hence the ironic
tourism phrase, 'Triabunna, where the forest meets the sea'.

Alf Cooper's place is at the end of a neat, quiet street. It's quite large –
classical seventies terracotta and white pillars, almost a Triabunna-style
grass castle. The entire frontage is paved but for four silver birch trees lined
up with military straightness along the picket fence. A white Daihatsu's
parked in one garage, a tarp-shrouded outboard boat in the other. Piles
of brown leaves under the boat suggest it's long retired. We knock, wait.
Nice sea tang to the air. When Alf Cooper opens the door he's struggling
into a shapeless cardy. His shorts expose skinny old legs terminating in a
pair of well-loved slippers. Alf is small and wizened, closer to eighty than
seventy-five, his skin pale and folded like a plucked turkey, but his eyes
are bright and alert, his snow-white body hairs sprightly. The air whiffs
faintly of unwashed elder citizen and a diet of fry-ups in vegetable fat.

'Alf Cooper? I'm Detective Inspector Franz Heineken, Major Crime
South, and this is Detective Rafe Tredway. Can we come in and ask you
a few questions, please?'

He stares intently at me, than at Rafe, then at our proffered IDs.

'Course ya can, gents.'

He leads us through a large, overheated, sparsely neat lounge-room, above the mantelpiece of which is a large framed image of a young boxer, into his kitchen, source, alas, of the fat odour. It's a neat kitchen, however.

'Was just boilin' the billy,' he says, flicking the switch on a kettle. 'Tea, gents? Bet you wanta know about them green bastards chained 'emselves to the woodchipper.'

'No, Mr Cooper. It's in connection with Moonah and Glenorchy Gloves, your old club.'

His leathery cancer-skinned hands come protectively up, as if we're a pair of ghastly ghost boxers. He peers in fright. He starts shaking his head. 'You lot don't give up, do ya? I swear I never burnt that place down! Youse tried to prove it, but ya proved nothing!' He takes a ragged breath, and he's starting to shake. Rafe steps in, puts a big young man's comforting hand on his bony shoulder.

'Easy on, Alf, we're not here about that. Just a question about a bloke who boxed there.'

'Oh?'

'Yeah, mate. Stan Fortune. Remember him?'

Alf Cooper nods, takes a few rasping breaths to try to calm himself. 'Stan – yeah ...'

'So you would know he was murdered, Mr Cooper, if you watch the news.'

He looks warily at me, nods again. 'So it *was* him, was it?'

'And we did ask the public to come forward with information. Did you not want to?'

'Jeez, didn't think about it that way. Didn't think I'd have anythin' useful to say, all this time on. He was just a tacker.'

He sits abruptly on a stool, puts a hand on his chest. 'Me heart's beatin' quick.'

'Take your time, Mr Cooper. Rafe, fix him his tea, would you? All we want to know, Mr Cooper, is who he boxed with, his mates at the club, if you can remember. But like I say, take your time, please.'

'Milk, sugar, mate?'

Cooper nods. Silence, but for the sounds of Rafe going about the chore. A moment for the old codger to get his wits back, to absorb the reality that we're not about to charge him for an insurance swindle that, for all I know, paid for this house and boat.

'That you above the mantelpiece in the lounge-room, Mr Cooper?'

'Yeah.'

'Lightweight?'

'In them early days, yeah. Welterweight later on.' He breathes in deeply, stands. 'I got pictures of 'em.'

'Good, that's very helpful.'

'Upstairs in one of me trunks. I'll go get 'em.'

'We'll wait in the lounge-room. Take his tea through, would you Rafe? After you Mr Cooper.'

Rafe and I hadn't said much on the journey here. In fact he seemed flat as a month-old road kill. He's rightly uneasy that we should be out here doing this when our man's already in the lockup, but he's held his tongue. Not least because of the poisonous political dimension to it regarding self and GTS. Now, in Cooper's large lounge-room, with its expansive water and woodchip views, we look at him framed in classic boxer's stance, the photo probably late fifties. Lots of smaller framed photos on the mantelpiece, mostly relatives, a couple of him and mates posing beside strung-up bluefin tuna. He'd have launched from the jetty here probably far more often than he dropped opponents to the canvas.

My mobile burrs. Quarry.

'Hello Wally.'

'G'day Franz, got a result for you on those missed messages to Fortune's home. All three phone calls were made from the public phone in the bar of the Strahan Hotel. That's your Tassie west coast Strahan, mate, not some place in Scotland. Sorry we didn't pick them up earlier.'

'No problem, it's an interesting result.'

'Glad to be of help, mate. See ya later.'

Cooper's coming back down the stairs, carrying a shoebox.

'What's up, boss?'

'Those phone calls to Fortune in Sydney were from Strahan.'

'Shit a brick.'

'Should be some in 'ere, gents.' Cooper sits at his dining room table and so do we. He takes an appreciative sip of his tea, nods thanks at Rafe. He seems to be over his shock, though he's still wary.

He takes off the lid of the shoebox, pulls out a handful of old photographs, some black and white, some an orangey faded colour. He clears his rheumy turkey-neck throat and begins to flick through them, casting some to one side, like he's a geriatric croupier setting up a game for a pair of menacing blow-ins to once-peaceful Triabunna. Finally, he's done. He sits back. 'There ya go, gents. Stan and his mates. They was four of them, best I ever had. They coulda been somebodies.'

He draws a breath, blinks a few times.

'Don't go all teary on us pop,' Rafe says, 'you're just becoming interesting.'

I scoop the ragged little pile towards me across the tabletop. The first photograph is a b&w, four young blokes posing face-on for the camera in their togs, boots and gloves. One could be Stan. I pass it to Rafe, take up the next, glance at it, pass it, the next, stop.

'Who's who, Mr Cooper?'

'Tell ya,' Rafe says, animatedly stabbing his finger onto a photo, 'That's Stan, that's his skull shape, recognise it anywhere.'

He'd know, having studied the X-ray showing the passage of the bullet.

'Me memory's sharp,' Alf Cooper volunteers. 'I knew and loved them boys and woulda done anythink for 'em, 'til it all went wrong.'

I find a larger image of the same four, place it near him, his side up. Rafe moves round behind him to see. Alf Cooper looks at it, sighs, says, 'My dream boys. My featherweight, lightweight, middleweight, heavyweight. Never was to be, gents, never was to be.' He rests a gnarly forefingernail on a face. 'Rob Pollard, my heavyweight.'

'Don't know him.' Or do I? The name rings a bell.

'Kelpie Rossiter, my welterweight.'

'No – keep going.'

'Jay Ho, my middleweight, my champ. Though Stan …'

He tears up again, the ancient coot, but we couldn't care less. Standing behind him Rafe throws a celebratory air pump. Not that we're going to say anything that Cooper might take down to the pub later on, namely that Jay Ho is well known to us. These days he owns Club Chillax, a Hobart waterfront nightclub that's a suspected player in the local amphetamine trade.

'Is Kelpie a nickname, Mr Cooper?'

'Uh … yeah, scrawny bugger. Jake Rossiter. Known to one and all as Kelpie.'

'What happened after the club went out of business?'

'They went and got in trouble with you lot, sadly. Growing and selling the noxious weed, they was – marryjiwana. Rob and Jay went in jail for it.'

'Why not Kelpie and Stan?'

He shrugs. 'Youse'll have your records on that, won't ya?'

'We will.'

'But I can tell ya,' he adds, 'why Stan shot through. Didn't seem in character to me, but I recall word got to Rob in Risdon Prison that Stan had, that he raped Rob's sister and broke her arm in the process.'

'Jeez!' Rafe says, sounding impressed, 'His big best mate's *sister?*'

Cooper nods gravely. 'Upset, Rob was. And so he let it be known that when he got out he'd be ripping Stan's head off his neck and shit in the cavity.'

'Friends no more!' Rafe grabs the pile of photos that apparently are no business of ours, begins flicking through them. 'Sure there's nothing in these for us, Alf?'

Cooper looks up at him. 'No.'

'I take it you've no objection to us borrowing these, Mr Cooper?' I gesture the ones he selected. 'Just for our records. They'll be returned soon.'

'No worries. Hadn't looked at 'em for years and years.'

'Have you anything else to tell us about this group?'

'Did one of 'em do the business on Stan? The TV said you arrested some other bloke.'

'Exactly so, Mr Cooper. We're just following all lines of inquiry.'

'Eliminating suspects,' Rafe adds.

'Nevertheless, Mr Cooper, you're required to keep this visit to yourself. If you don't, and I find out, you'll be up for disobeying a police instruction.'

'In which case your days in this house could be over, mate.' Rafe peers appreciably around the lounge-room, nods at the view through the large windows. 'Really nice place to have bought on a boxing trainer's wage.'

'My oath, gents, no one's gunna know a word of this. I generally keep to meself anyway.'

'Good.' I stand. 'Thanks for your help, Mr Cooper. We'll see ourselves out.'

RAFE EXECUTES A RAPID THREE-POINT AND SHOOTS US AWAY WITH customary hoonlike acceleration. 'So what do you reckon, boss? Jay bloody Ho. Be nice to pin a big one on that slippery bastard.'

'Early days, Rafe. Twenty-plus years is a long time.' I use the car phone. 'Faye, Franz.'

'Hi boss, hi Rafe. How did you go?'

'Run a check on these names, Rob Pollard and Jake Rossiter, latter commonly known as Kelpie. Both early fifties. Also an update on Jay Ho. Their histories back as far as you can. They're the MAGG boxers. Stan's old mates.'

'Will do boss. Where are you?'

'Approaching Orford, but the way Rafe's driving you can put our ETA down as ten minutes.'

She laughs, but says, 'Don't arrive as statistics. Out.'

'Actually, boss, I need a slash if that's okay.' He pulls exuberantly in alongside an Orford takeaway, hops out, strides into the gents. I know what'll happen next. Sure enough, straight from the gents into the joint and out with a pie. He puts it on the centre console and accelerates away.

'Didn't think you'd want one,' he says.

I don't bother to reply. I can smell the industrial-strength tomato sauce he would have injected liberally into it, and he'll be wondering how long he can wait before biting into it without burning his gob. They say that if we non-abattoir types knew what was in most pies we wouldn't eat them. But given that the national cuisine is a warm pie in one hand and a cold beer in the other, eaten consumed while shoutily watching sport, a pastry-cased sludge of mince, sugar and salt washed down with cheap piss can't be all bad.

WE'VE JUST CROSSED THE MUNICIPAL BOUNDARY BETWEEN GLAMORGAN-Spring Bay and Tasman when Faye calls in.

'Jay Ho and Rob Pollard each did time for trafficking a commercial quantity of marijuana when they were in their twenties.'

'Old news, mate,' Rafe replies.

'Stan Fortune and Kelpie Rossiter were named but got off on a technicality. Pollard seems to be a nasty piece of work. He's twice been inside for GBH, and was also convicted of assaulting his de facto. The file record also says he's a, quote, "authority-hater".'

'Read "us",' Rafe says.

'Pollard was a dog breeder in the midlands until quite recently. Now he lives on a smallholding south of Dunalley. He –'

'Faye. Stop. What kind of dogs?'

'Not sure, boss.'

'Find out. And if he lives near Dunalley he's likely to be intimately familiar with the Tasman Peninsula.'

'Oh shit yes, the beach where Stan was buried.'

'Exactly. And if he bred hunting dogs that would make him a hunter himself, a user of deer bags. What about Rossiter?'

'Um … okay.' We hear the rustle of paperwork. 'Kelpie Rossiter's a charter boat operator. He's been licensed for twenty years, though he spent five driving heavy duty trucks in the Kalgoorlie and Coolgardie gold mines. A cleanskin, though, from the little I've found so far.'

'What's his home port?'

'Strahan, boss – lovely, faraway, isolated Strahan.'

12

UNPREDICTED, THEREFORE ENTIRELY EXPECTED, DRIVING SLEET SHEETS
over the back of the black mountain like a white blanket. Hobart
freezes for half an hour, then sunshine melts it away in the blink of an
unbelieving eye, the southerly turned by the northerly. And we cops
are just as at sixes and sevens. Myself, I'm darkly annoyed. But also
vindicated. That trip to Sydney is paying dividends. We've pinged
the wrong man and a video hook-up with Taylor Square is about
to prove that. Gillian Yinakis phoned last night, not ten minutes
after I'd put the light out. As pyjama news goes it was nothing less
than extraordinary, requiring a response from the very top of the
organisation to which I belong.

Hunt, D'Hayt, self, Hunt's media PA, Hedda, and her Drug Branch
boss John Petrie make up our complement. On their side, Gillian Yinakis,
her boss, the NSW Assistant Commissioner Crime, and two others. The
four of them angle down at us from the giant plasma screen. It would
hardly surprise me if Gillian Yinakis transmuted and joined us at our
table. We've made our greetings. She's asked which news we want first,
the bad or the worse. I've suggested chronology.

'Okay, here we go,' she says, her soft voice compellingly clear in the
perfect silence of Hunt's lair. 'Contrary to his happy-go-lucky barman
image, Stan Fortune has brought a fair amount of grief to all of us. Until
now he's been your mysterious dead body. And until now he's had no
connection to my two ongoing problems, a corrupt drug enforcement
unit and bikie warfare. Stupid Stan lit a fuse firing up both.'

'Glad to hear it,' Hunt says. 'Grief shared is grief halved.'

'Stan was for many years an informant for the longest serving detective
in our drug squad, one of the old school, Hugh Hughes.'

I don't chip in to say that I 'know' the big wavy grey-haired boofhead
who in a lift raised his eyes skyward at the mention of her name.

'Stan consistently and reliably provided Hugh Hughes with good information from where he worked, that is, bars associated with the illicit substance industry. And I'm told that Stan was of a type to not ever become suspect among his peers. So he brought rewards for Hugh, but Hugh grew lazy on them, because, in return for solid information, for example enabling a successful raid on a minor drug factory, Hugh got brownies and Stan got dollars from our COF, our Covert Operations Fund. With no proper record-keeping.'

She pauses, sips water. 'Franz, you will know that Stan was going to be turfed from his job. And that his girl had left him. And that he couldn't crack the Revs.'

'I do.'

'Which left him in a difficult personal situation. He therefore asked Hugh Hughes for a golden handshake, namely one hundred thousand dollars, for services rendered over many years. Hugh brought the request to me. I'd been head of the branch for two weeks. I couldn't wait to crack down on the old school of slipping cash to slippery informants. But it was something I inherited. And, worse, at the time, Hugh's snitch was known only to himself, with full internal legal impunity for that. I reluctantly agreed thirty grand. The last ever such payout under my watch. And I only authorised this one because Stan had apparently threatened Hugh that he'd otherwise go public with names of other informants known to him.'

She rubs the back of her neck. Here comes the really bad news.

'Hugh Hughes gave Stan the cash. Stan was very pissed off. He called it a bronze handshake and said he'd be making up the difference elsewhere. Which he did. Hugh had earlier let slip to Stan that the Drags had just established a new drug warehouse in Sutherland, a fact known to very few. And Hugh also told him the day on which all the Drags would be at Cronulla Beach with Deng Xien and that they would be arrested. So Stan hatched his ghastly little plan. He pulled in a few Revs and they raided the Sutherland house. Stan helped himself to a million dollar's worth of cocaine and relocated to Tasmania. Why do I know this? Because we have been monitoring Hugh. Listen, Stan speaks first, with the fast voice.'

Gillian Yinakis presses the switch of a recorder on the table in front of her.

'Hello mate it's me how's it going mate?'

'What the bloody hell do you want?'

'Hey, be nice mate, just thought I'd let you know something, that pissy

104

bronze handshake mate? I got resourceful and turned it to gold. Thanks to you funny enough.'

'What the fuck are you talking about?'

'Loose lips mate you really shouldn't have told me about Sutherland.'

'What? Don't make me laugh you maggot, you couldn't arrange a piss-up in a fucking brewery.'

'Then why do I have a kilo of finest Colombian marching powder in my suitcase mate?'

'You're talking shit. Where are you anyway?'

'Die wondering mate.'

'You're *dead!*'

'Ooroo Hughsey!'

The audible click marking the end of that conversation hangs in the air like a bad smell.

'Christ.' Hunt just about fists the table. 'It would have helped to know this before now.'

'I'm not apologising,' Yinakis retorts. 'We didn't know the identity of Stan until Franz gave me the details of the mobile found in his suitcase in Hobart. We traced that mobile to Hughes. It had been issued to him from the COF, which is why it was untraceable through our normal channels. As to the murder, well Hughes flatly denies putting word out that Stan was an informant. He knows he's in enough trouble without having an incitement to murder charge thrown in.'

Hedda's turf. She says, 'I'd not be so sure about that, Gill. I worked with Hugh for long enough to know that he takes his grudges seriously. But there's also this. One suspect here runs nightclubs and that likely means a cocktail of drugs – and as we all know, that therefore means organised crime somewhere along the chain. A word from Hugh would get here quickly enough, and he'd have known that, I reckon.'

'Do you have reliable informants who might be able to confirm that? I'm ready to hang and quarter him.'

'I've asked certain parties to ask around, yes.'

'Does the name Jay Ho mean anything to you, Gillian?' Hunt watches her expectantly.

'No. Why?'

'He's a party of interest in our local drug scene, and he has a distant connection to Stan.'

'We'll run a check.' She makes a note. 'And that's about it, Grif. Hopefully this new, uh … *angle* will assist you. Something for you to get your teeth into, Hedda!'

'You're dead right it will, Gill, leave it to us aggressive pointyheads to sort out your problems.'

Stiff chuckles, goodbyes. And as they blip into nothingness, we collectively shift, pause for thought. Hunt sits back, laces hands behind head, talks. 'Two strategies. One, a decision on Athol Burden. Two, trace the cocaine.'

He might look relaxed, but those laced hands are to stop him throwing something at the plasma screen.

John Petrie's never been one to miss an opportunity. 'So,' he says to Walter, 'You've charged some flea-ridden bogan with murder because he shoots ferals and now you want the cavalry to come and clear it all up.' He and Hedda smile broadly. It's a straight case of one-upmanship played out in front of the boss.

'Believe me, you would have done exactly the same,' Walter says.

As far as retorts go it's a stinker, even by his standards. It's a wonder Hunt doesn't burst out laughing. All he does is sigh, and propel himself forward, elbows on the desk. My turn.

'Well then, Franz,' he says. 'Thanks to your persistence we may just have the lead we need to take this forward. First things first. In your opinion, given what we now know, could Burden still be the guilty party?'

'No. But I'd advise that we keep him until such time as we can eliminate him from having any connection with whoever went after the cocaine, including Ho and company.'

'That could solve a short-term problem,' Hunt says. 'Walter?'

Walter nods. 'I guess so. We'll be crucified in the media if we just let him go.'

'And that will alert our new suspects.'

'Right. Franz, Hedda, I guess you're a team again.'

She looks at me, says to all, 'I'll keep a tight lead on DI Heineken.'

Laughter. It's a relief of tension. None except Rafe know that we're occasional partners. Some may have an inkling. Let them inkle away.

'I'd like a result on this ASAP,' Hunt goes on. 'I'm not holding my breath, but it would be nice, given the hole we've dug for ourselves. So, let's have chapter and verse on these three, please Franz.'

'Our starting point needs to be this, that there is nothing to suggest that Jay Ho, Rob Pollard and Kelpie Rossiter maintain any kind of relationship. What they did twenty years ago with Stan Fortune does not magically translate into a solution for us. So I'm assuming nothing. But they have form. I'll go through the files on each.'

Faye has done a good job finding and chronologically ordering information on them, and she's managed to get hold of some relatively recent halfway decent mugshots. I start with Jay Ho. Three A4 colour images. He's of medium build, early fifties, intelligent-looking, seems to favour white or cream suits without ties.

'He was born in Hong Kong to a Chinese father and a white Australian mother and he grew up in Melbourne and then Hobart. You all know about them as a boxing quartet and their subsequent move into the marijuana trade. Ho did eighteen months in Risdon for his part in it. He and Fortune had been the salesmen, Fortune locally, Ho interstate. A much bigger market, but exposing him to greater risk. Proved his undoing. Since then he's been in the entertainment industry, here and in Melbourne. He owns Club Chillax outright and part-owns two Melbourne outer suburban nightclubs. There's no doubt that he's a supplier of ice and GHB for Chillax patrons, but he's clever, keeps his hands clean. We haven't been able to touch him.'

The file on Rob Pollard's also fairly comprehensive. The most recent image of him is vaguely disturbing. He had been a long-time hunting dog breeder in the Midlands. That was until three years ago, when two of his dogs attacked him. He managed to fend them off and then shot them, but not before they'd had a good go at him, getting stuck into one leg and his torso. He limps now. And he also received a raking bite to the right side of his face, removing most of the eyebrow and leaving three nasty scars on his cheek. No more dogs for big bad Rob. He has since claimed disability benefit. It was from this that Faye got his mugshot and a full body shot of his wounds. No wonder he gave the dogs away. Both naked and clothed he's a formidable sight, tall, heavy in the upper body, great big square jaw, filthy-looking expression, aggressive moustache, number 2 cropped grey-flecked hair showing a large skull.

'Charming,' is Hunt's assessment.

'Pollard's always been rural. He used to drive into town to the boxing club from a smallholding near New Norfolk and it was there that he began growing the commercial quantities of marijuana that Ho and Fortune sold. Once the enterprise brought solid returns he purchased a bigger block in the north-west to take advantage of the better growing conditions. As the owner of that block it was easy to get a conviction for him. He did two-and-a-half years and has since been back inside twice for serious assault and he was also found guilty of assaulting his then de facto. All up he's a nasty piece of work, and a dedicated cop hater. And the deer lodge owner, Charlie Pennington, marked him at the top of his list, even though he'd left the district.'

Kelpie Rossiter is last. We know least about him. His mugshot's possibly ten years old, the only image of him Faye could find, and we all have a long, fascinated look at it on the table.

'Skinny bugger.'

'Yeah, not much of him.'

'Aboriginal?'

'Could be … and bloody hell, he's kept the local tatts artist busy.'

Kelpie Rossiter's standing in the stern of a fishing cruiser, alongside a large strung-up bluntnose sixgill shark. He's wearing tight salt-faded old jeans and nothing else. One hand is flat against the fish's dull chocolatey flank, the other holds a stubby. He's looking at the camera with an expression somewhere between easy triumph and deadly arrogance, and he pulls it off because his toned, sculpted frame supports a face of film star attractiveness: slightly elongated, dark golden beard, tangles and tendrils of windswept hair down to his shoulders. But the leading man comparison's a fleeting one. A rollie dangles from his lip. Tattoos of sea serpents, mermaids and sharks cover most of his visible flesh, from belly button to neck, both arms. Cover them up and he's the coolest fisho you ever saw. Expose them and the narrative's not quite the same.

I read out what little there is about him. 'Kelpie Rossiter's role was to transport the marijuana. He grew up in a fishing family and seems to have always had a boat. The prosecution case was that he took the processed dope from the New Norfolk site downstream on the Derwent and distributed it from there, and that as the operation developed he began ferrying from the north-west across Bass Strait. But that couldn't be proved, so he didn't do time. But whereas Fortune went interstate, Rossiter moved back to Strahan and looked after the monetary proceeds on behalf of Ho and Pollard while they were inside.'

'Jesus, that was good of him!'

'Or cautious of him. He would have been well aware of Pollard's threat to kill Fortune. Whatever the case, he must have looked after himself as well, because the word out west is that he's a seriously wealthy bloke. Dodgy, though. No one quite knows where the money keeps coming from.'

'Wouldn't be the first.'

'No. We do know that he spent time working in the goldfields of Kalgoorlie and Coolgardie, driving heavy vehicles. That would have made him a fair whack. Interestingly, he returned to Tassie just at the time when those police raids closed down the Ennapinka Field.'

'Ah.' Hunt's interested. His WA counterpart had taken the drastic step of trying to curb a serious drug culture in the mines. Lots of cash attracting lots of high grade cocaine in one of the world's boom zones. 'Rossiter, with his trade knowledge, could have been a courier or a go-between.'

'Possibly.'

'And what does he do with himself in Strahan?'

'Ostensibly he's a big-game fisherman. He does advertise for well-heeled clients, and he gets them, but very much on his own terms. He operates for just three months in the year, for instance. So presumably he doesn't need to work to live.'

'Family man?'

'Wife, one adult daughter, and girlfriends in every port by the sound of it. The intrigue for us is why he set out in his cruiser in atrocious, dangerous weather just two days, give or take, before Fortune's death. He told his wife he was going marlin fishing off the east coast. My theory is that he slipped down to Hobart to pick up the cocaine. That was seventeen days ago. His boat's not been back at its Strahan tie-up. We can't speak to the wife for fear of her alerting him, but the word from our blokes in Strahan is that they have a pretty casual relationship, that she'll say to her hairdressing clients she hasn't the faintest idea where Kelpie is. What is definite is that, like him, she sleeps around.'

'Lucky locals. So where *is* Kelpie?'

'My hope is that Pollard and Ho are in touch with him.'

'We'll not be doing any electronic surveillance, Franz. Not while we only have conjectures and theories. Take it to the next level and come back to me.'

'I'll do that, Grif.'

13

THE THING ABOUT SANDY BAY, AS FAR AS BAYS GO, IS IT'S NOT THAT sandy and there's not much bay. Bunged up with millionaires, home to Australia's first casino, a university, sexual playground of the teenage Errol Flynn when the twentieth century was young, 'The Bay' does not equal crime. Whether inside a car or walking along the pleasant riverside boulevard, you can't see the expanse of Jay Ho's Sandy Bay Road property. It hides behind a thick and leaning three-metre high sandstone wall, probably built by convicts in the dwindling years of transportation. But the electronic gate gives a hint of something other than wealth. Down here at forty-two degrees south very few individuals feel the need to lock themselves away from their well-heeled neighbours.

'What a knob,' Rafe says, buttoning down his driverside window and pushing the buzzer on the intercom. 'Watching us as well.'

I know that. The CCTV's hidden inside a small faux, make that crass, gargoyle mounted on top of the high gate. Not that well hidden. A male voice says, 'Yeah?'

'Jay Ho?'

'Who is it?'

Rafe holds his patience. 'Are you Jay Ho?'

The voice doesn't. 'I'm asking who the fuck you are, mate!'

Rafe sighs, pulls out his ID, holds it hard against the windscreen so the CCTV can get a good look at it. 'Police,' he says, adds with mock civility,' And whoever *you* are, sir, open the gate please.'

Silence of the stunned kind from the intercom, so much so that I swear I heard the voice's eyes widen.

The gate slides into the rack bolted to the inside of the thick sandstone wall. In we go. The driveway curves along a large overgrown garden with mature trees. Knowing what we know about Jay Ho, I'm betting there's no honest garden soil under his fingernails.

'Am I wrong, Rafe, or is he an ostentatious bastard as well as a knob?'

'Too right, boss. Like some bloody ambassador's place, for Christ's sake.'

The driveway's demarcated on each side by a chain-link fence, about half a metre above the manicured grass, the single chains held up by metal bollards so that they form graceful, make that hideous, loops. But we see a funnier side as we pull up in front of the two-storey house. A pair of skid marks have chewed up the lawn, taking out a section of this fence. Uprooted bollards lie about.

Rafe laughs. 'Scenario, boss. Jay or one of his mates, showing off, pissed and or stoned, slams his wheels into reverse and doesn't realise just how much stallion's under the bonnet.'

There's a bell, brass, bold, set into the large door. My knock is also bold. Never been a doorbelly kind of person.

And here he is, in his trademark white suit sans tie. Apricot shirt with enough buttons undone to display a khaki-skinned, hairless chest. Gold cufflinks. Deck shoes. He's about 190 in height, medium build and, now that I know this, he has the build and poise of a middleweight. No one ever got his nose, though, so he must have been reasonably smart on his pins. His eyes are the colour of green olives. One of them's stuffed with a pimento – it's got a bloodshot orb – but we know this feature from his most recent mugshot when he was unsuccessfully charged with dealing about six years ago. And it now occurs to me that it's possibly boxing-related.

'Good morning, gents. What can I do for you?' He looks relaxed and he's smiling lightly.

'Hello, Mr Ho. I'm DI Franz Heineken and this is Detective Tredway. Can we come in?' I show my ID. Rafe doesn't bother. He already did.

Ho thinks about it. Not that he has much choice. To decline will only invite suspicion. 'Sure,' he says, stepping back inside. 'Will it take long? I've got business in town pretty soon.'

Rafe, ever the gentleman, waves me to precede him. We enter a small portico, the original purpose of which would have been for the landed gentry to hang up coats and brollies and to scrape and wipe mud from riding boots. Then a short flight of steps at the top of which is a long and wide passageway. Ho hops up these steps. I follow his deck shoes.

'Been renovating, mate?' Rafe asks.

There was, until recently by the look of it, a passageway carpet. The air smells faintly of the exposed stone floor and carpet glue, and there are popped carpet tacks here and there, small, and in cracks between neatly fitted bluestone slabs. You wouldn't normally notice. But the Tasmanian taxpayer pays us to notice.

'Didn't like the colour, to be honest,' Ho replies equably.

'And who renovated your lawn and driveway chain, mate?' Rafe laughs. Ho grins awkwardly, says, 'That's one guest never coming back,' and leads us into a kind of ante lounge-room. It has a direct mountain view. I can imagine this small room having been purposely built for its view, the large single window exaggerating the closeness of Mount Wellington's Organ Pipes, a dolerite sound system hanging sheer down the face in your face, so to speak.

He turns, waits.

'Mr Ho, I'd like to ask you some questions about Stan Fortune.'

'Oh ... Stan. Jeez, poor bloke.' Ho shakes his head sadly.

'You're obviously aware that it took us some time to identify him?'

'Yeah, sure. And well done. Good work.'

'And after we identified him, we continued to ask the public to come forward with anything that might help us. So why didn't you?'

Ho looks away, briefly, then back at me, Rafe, me. 'Shit, sorry. I mean, it never crossed my mind. I'd only known him bloody years and years ago, when we were kids basically.' He seems a mite relieved, as if he's hoping this is the purpose of our visit. To scold him for not telling us they boxed and peddled drugs decades ago.

'So when last did you see him?' Rafe asks.

Ho's been waiting for that, barely needs to sway out of its range.

'Oh, mate, must be twenty, twenty-five years ago I reckon.'

'After you got out of jail back then?'

'No, mate, he'd left Tassie by then. So it would have been before.'

'Okay.' I nod. Ho looks hopefully at me, as if that's all we can logically ask, and he's passed. But Jay Ho's a smart bloke and he knows very well that's never the case. So he's playing innocent citizen. I don't like such games at the best of times.

'Did he ever contact you from Sydney, Mr Ho?'

'Uh ... No. Not that I recall.'

'Have you ever spoken to anyone about him recently, or has anyone spoken to you about him recently?'

'Jeez, again, no.'

'Are you sure?'

He frowns, thinking hard, takes the plunge. 'Mate, uh inspector, I just don't reckon I can be of any help to you. I mean, that's why I never contacted you blokes, like I said. And, you know, that bloke you've locked up, don't know who the hell he is, if that's what you're asking.'

Rafe's mobile rings. He grabs it, whirls about, off like a shot. I don't know who's calling, but I know where he's going.

'Do you know why he left Tasmania?'

The question surprises him.

'Uh ...' He frowns, as if recollecting hard. Maybe he is. Then he smiles. 'Stan avoided going inside. I reckon he pissed off before you blokes could have had another crack at him!'

I chuckle, nod. We hear the front door close. Ho glances at the passageway, back at me. 'Just pathetic,' he says. 'Sure, we did a bit of grass, but the Stan I knew was a good bloke, never would want to do anyone any harm, you know? The last person you'd expect someone would just, you know, shoot the poor bastard in the back of the head like that.'

'People change, Mr Ho.'

'Yeah, guess so.'

Rafe comes back in. 'Sorry about that, boss.'

I'd like him to have heard what I've just heard, as a witness, but I don't think it matters in the scheme of things. What matters is that Ho said it.

'Would you think Stan Fortune would have been capable of running with outlaw motorcycle gangs, Mr Ho?'

He laughs. 'If anyone told you that I reckon it's bullshit! Stan was a good boxer but a softie.'

'Bullshit is usually half true,' Rafe reminds him.

'Yeah but mate, what I know of bikies is they're hard as.'

'Okay. Just one more question then, Mr Ho. We know that you did time back then with Rob Pollard, and that Kelpie Rossiter, like Stan Fortune, was an interested party in the crime for which you and Pollard were jailed. Do you keep up with Pollard or Rossiter?'

'Uh, not in a regular way, no. I'm a city slicker and those boys are well and truly country folk.' He smiles happily at us.

'When last were you in touch with Rob?'

'Oh, mate, we get together for a beer now and again. I mean, once or twice a year max, maybe he pulls into town, drops by.'

'So the last occasion was ...?'

'Good six months ago? To be honest, I couldn't exactly tell you off the top of my head. I do a lot of socialising, you know.'

We know.

'And what about Kelpie?'

'Nah, less still. I think he's still fishing on the west coast. Strahan. Born a west coaster and he'll die a west coaster.'

He watches carefully as I take one of my cards from my wallet, hand it to him. 'For your collection, Mr Ho. And in case you remember something and want to contact me.'

Jay Ho smiles a smile that seems to be trying not to convey exactly what it is, namely, relief, lingering uncertainty, and just a touch of the smugness that goes with the territory upon which his kind strut their stuff.

'No worries.' He looks at the card. 'Thanks, Mr Heineken.'

'Thank you too, Mr Ho. I'm sure you understand that we have to follow all lines of inquiry, even though an arrest has been made.'

'It's procedure,' Rafe adds.

Ho watches us to the car. I hear the front door close as I get into the passenger seat, on the floor of which is one of the link-chain bollards. It's a smooth metal pipe about three quarters of a metre in length, with a fat blob of cement at one end, the end embedding it in the ground until the thing got yanked out. I pick it up. It fits nicely in the hand, is hollow, the cement blob a decent endweight.

'That's not all, boss.' Rafe accelerates down the snaking driveway. 'I had a look at the bottom of the stairs just on the edge where the carpet was taken up, and against the wall there are faint marks. I can tell you, mate, they have haemoglobin rings marking them out as stains.'

'Could we get a DNA sample?'

'You can see they've been scrubbed. But they're blood. Trust me, boss.'

'I've no reason not to. And I have something too. When you were gone he got on a bit of a roll and he wondered who'd, quote, "shoot the poor bastard in the back of the head", unquote.'

'Holy shit! What he's not supposed to know!' Rafe enters Sandy Bay Road and aims us at the CBD. The first thing we need to do is have another look at the forensic report. That is, after we've diverted to Pollard's place. South of Dunalley, it's less than an hour away.

THE NARROW AND WINDING TASMAN HIGHWAY, ALTERNATING BETWEEN olde world and thirde world, delivers us into the township of Dunalley, notable for its bakery and the canal that lets fishing and leisure boats shortcut the Tasman Peninsula. Pollard's acreage is fifteen minutes further along. Make that nine if you're Det. Tredway at the wheel of

114

a Ford Falcon Turbo Sedan with a mere 750 ks on the odo. The extent of Pollard's place is hard to judge. It's tucked in against a densely wooded hillside, and the road in, rutted and angular, is suitably in keeping with the hand-painted gate sign, *keep out enter at you'r own risk.*

The solid timber house looks quiet. We get out. The front yard's messy, blokey. A dead ute, stacks of firewood, planks, rope. A black Toyota LandCruiser Prado VX Wagon with big boofheaded roo bars and hunting lights sits in the carport. From a chimney grey tendrils of the smoke of a long-lit fire lift thinly into a morose sky. Mizzle rain has just begun to fall, steals over us, bringing a distinct new cold with it. Our breathing's fogged. It's quiet. Too quiet, as they say in the B-grades.

I knock loudly. We wait on a raised verandah that wraps around the whole place. Knock again.

'Check out the back would you Rafe?'

He clumps along the verandah, hops off, disappears.

I knock a third time, then begin peering through windows. Nothing of interest – if you take away the motheaten-looking deer heads on the walls.

A kookaburra, somewhere unseen, breaks the silence. And my mobile answers it.

'Hello Faye.'

'Hi, boss, this is really good. A call just came in about the Port Jackson Movers van. A lady says she definitely saw it in her street. She described it really well, though not the actual name. Interstate plates, right colour, no windows, and she put a date on it that's just about what we want, when Fortune died. It was parked in her street.'

'Why so good?'

'I thought you'd say that, sir.' Faye titters. She knows when she's onto a hot lead, keeping in step with the prickly one's innate sense of suspicion about 'definite' information. 'She's a past president of the Sandy Bay Retirees' Association and she's got this thing about traffic. Apparently a roundabout's planned near Hutchins School and she thinks this is going to divert traffic towards the new old age home and endanger its low care residents who like to walk to the reserve. So she's been logging the traffic every third day she says, for an hour, and noting the volume – whether car, motorbike, small truck, big truck. And the thing is, she does it from the sunroom of her house, which is the street behind Jay Ho's place.'

Rafe's back and doing his version of window-peering.

'That's quality, Faye. Did she ring or come in?'

'Rang.'

'Shoot over to her and organise an affidavit. Now, if you can.'

'Will do, boss. Are you at Pollard's place?'

'Yes.' I pocket the mobile. We stand together on the boards, looking back down the enter-at-your-own-risk track, dragon-like fog puffs coming from us, and I'm pretty sure Rafe's feeling the same persistent, nagging unease about this place that I am.

In the big, forested damp silence we're having a cop moment.

We're being watched.

Not much to be done about it. I take out one of my cards, write on it, *Please call me*, date it, and wedge the card firmly into the jamb of the front door.

Rafe executes a three-point on the tatty wet grass. 'What do you reckon boss?'

'Either of these two, Rafe. His dunny's deep in the bush and he's constipated, or Ho gave him a hoi, as a result of which he's not keen to talk to us.'

'They'll be wanting to get their story straight first.'

'Exactly. To sing from the same songsheet, in the words of the immortal GTS. So we can anticipate them getting together. But let's start by finding out if he was at home, was watching us ...'

We're at the gate, open as we left it and how it can stay, seeing as he was rude enough not to respect our courtesy call.

'Find a park hidden from view. Let's see if we've flushed him.'

Rafe zips us along for a short while, we bounce off the bitumen and he does a neat donut and reverses us at speed into a small gap in a tangle of eucalypts and coastal wattle. And so we wait. I put the radio on, for the local news. A tugboat nearly smacked into the Tasman Bridge. Another so-called sighting of a so-called thylacine, this one by a pair of Swedish tourists described as reliable. Better than expected unemployment figures. And a nasty cold front on the way, with rain, sleet, snow.

'How can people still think the tiger's out there?' Rafe taps the side of his head.

'Maybe it is.'

'You serious?'

'Maybe it's doing a Rob Pollard on us.'

'Yeah, right ...'

I feed myself an allsort, tune out of the low voice of the *Country Hour* host droning the virtues of the kipfler potatoes from the chocolate soils of the north-west. Where the Swedes saw their tiger, on a forestry road between Smithton and the Arthur River. Rafe's got the wipers on intermittent. Very few cars.

'So how long do you want to wait?'

'Half an hour.'

'Okay.'

But Rafe's an impatient boy, and he soon begins to shift about.

'I reckon he would have moved by now, boss.'

'Ten more minutes.'

We wait.

Text message. Nora. She's thinking of coming for Christmas after all. Will the shack be free? Good. I'll enjoy seeing her again.

'Hey, boss?'

'Yes?'

'What's a tourist say after visiting the Tasman Peninsula?'

'I don't know, Rafe, what's a tourist say after visiting the Tasman Peninsula?'

'Nubeena there, Dunalley that.'

We wait.

His stomach growls. He stretches, scratches, clears his throat loudly, changes to an FM channel, knows I don't like fluffy pop music, back to the *Country Hour*.

Twenty-five minutes. An ancient truck loaded with firewood staggers into view, headed north.

'Okay, Rafe. Go.' I don't want to be stuck behind its diesel fumes. Rafe drops the handbrake and we shoot onto the road. He accelerates and we surge, but even so, the swiftly receding truck driver flashes us. Rafe puts his rude finger against the rear view mirror.

Sure enough, as we turn into Dunalley's main drag off the canal bridge, Rafe says, 'I reckon the bakery needs my custom, boss. Get you anything?'

'Can't you wait until we get back? Eat in the canteen like everyone else?'

'Mate, come on, they make the best scallop pies in the southern hemisphere.'

'Be quick.'

He swings across and off the road, gets out and bounds into the place. Arms folded, I'm looking in my doorside mirror for the firewood truck. I don't like diesel fumes at the best of times. Rafe didn't think of that, did he? And I didn't think that I'd see in the mirror, not the truck,

117

but Rob Pollard's Prado. Instinctively I hunch a bit. The speed limit's 40 kph and he's sticking to it, so I get a fair look at him as he drives past. He's on his mobile, doesn't appear to recognise our car. Even in this brief sighting his bulk is evident. So are the scars on the side of his large, grim face.

I watch the Prado accelerate up the incline that will take it out of Dunalley. Rafe gets back in with his pie and a Pepsi. He's seen it too. And we've got a job now, tailing Pollard. What chance he'll be aiming for, say, Club Chillax?

14

STUFF TO LAY ON HUNT. AND WALTER HAS TAGGED ALONG, BUBBLING
and fuming away. Back in the big man's lair so soon, eh, but now just the
four of us, because this is no mere meeting, it's a hardball get and the
stakes are higher than going for a speccy in the goalsquare at the death
with a point in it.

'Franz, this had better be good.' Hunt's seriously close to pissed off
with me, because Walter has got in his ear and told him that what I have
is dubious. I'm not worried. For me, Athol is Walter's burden and he's
welcome to him.

'It *is* good, Grif. One, Rob Pollard is or was a deer hunter. Stags
mounted on the wall of his house confirm that and they're not recent
trophies. It surely means he was in the business a long time ago, so he might
well have owned an old deer bag of the type used to bury Fortune. Two, he
hid from us this morning. Why? Because Ho must have phoned him ...'

'Wait up, Franz.'

'What is it, Walter?'

'You don't have proof that he hid from you.'

Rafe snorts. Walter glares at him. I'll keep talking.

'We tailed Pollard and, as we thought, he drove straight to Club
Chillax. A few minutes later he and Ho came out of the club, got into
Ho's 370Z and they drove off. Unfortunately we lost them.'

'How did you manage to do that?'

'Ho jumped two ambers in Davey Street. I wasn't prepared to chase.
No point bailing them up until we've decided our strategy.'

'Okay, go on.'

'As for Jay Ho, his house is ground zero, we're convinced of that. We
believe Fortune met his end there. Rafe?'

Rafe has an evidence bag next to his chair. He takes out the bollard,
places it on the table. 'There are a number of these lying around at Ho's

place,' he says. 'Inside the front door a set of four steps leads up to a passageway that was carpeted until recently. This is what DI Heineken and me reckon happened.'

Rafe stands, takes up the bollard in one hand. 'Fortune was bludgeoned to the back of the head with something that left cement grains in the wound.' He rubs the cement blob at one end of the bollard. Grains come away in his fingertips. 'And when Fortune was smacked the force of it propelled him down a set of stairs. Doctor Doll's pathology report records four distinct bruise lines across the torso and legs, consistent with falling hard onto carpeted steps.'

Now Rafe steps away from the table and holds the bollard lightly, testing its weight, the smoothness of the pipe. He looks convincing. Maybe because in summer he plays cricket, opening the bowling for a social team. The fact that the game's a six-hour excuse for a seven-hour piss-up is neither here nor there. Just for now, Rafe looks the goods.

'So, Mr Hunt, we reckon Jay Ho and Rob Pollard have got Stan Fortune in that house, and things have gone bad for Stan, like he's done this coke deal with them and now they've found out he was an informant. They're in the lounge-room, accusing Stan. Rob's holding one of these, to show they mean business. Stan's shitting himself, trying to bluff his way out of it. But he knows it's no good, so he suddenly turns and legs it along the passageway, towards the front door. Rob Pollard's a big, powerful bloke, a mad bastard. This is his kind of game, pursuing the quarry. So he steps forward, winds up his throwing arm with the bollard.'

Rafe acts it out and we instinctively tense up. 'He probably shouts something like "*Cop this!*" and lets fly. Crunch. A good hit, right in the back of the head.

'Fortune crashes down the steps like a sack of spuds, smashing his nose. And there he lies, concussed, bleeding heavily from the head wound and the nose. Ho and Pollard panic. Fortune looks dead, but perhaps he moves a bit. So one of them shoots him through the back of the skull. They strip him of his ID, though they miss the keys around his neck, put him in a deer bag that Pollard had in his Prado, drive to that beach and bury him. Up comes the carpet. And they've also done something with Fortune's van and bike that we don't know about. Could be in the bush at Pollard's.'

'And,' I add, 'let's not forget that Ho referred to him being shot in the back of the head. And there are the phone calls made to Fortune's Sydney house from Strahan, right after Fortune and his pals robbed the Drags' drug warehouse. Putting Kelpie Rossiter in the frame as well.'

Rafe sits. Hunt contemplates it all.

'Compelling, gentlemen, no doubt about that. But you're riding on assumptions rather than hard evidence. And assumptions won't get me a warrant to go into that house and test for a blood match. Especially not while we've got Burden locked up.'

'I'd like to keep them under surveillance, Grif. We can do that at least, and I think it's worth doing. They're uneasy. They might lead us somewhere, to something. The hard evidence you need.'

'Alright, you've got forty-eight hours. After that, we proceed with the case against Burden.'

FORTY-EIGHT HOURS IS A TOKEN GESTURE IN THIS BUSINESS, AND IT will take a fair slab of luck to swing the wind my way. At least we'll be following a simple plan. We being the five in my office early the next morning, self, Rafe, Faye, Hedda and Troy.

'This is how we'll do it,' I say. 'Troy, you go and park yourself on the south side of Dunalley. If, hopefully when, Pollard drives past, follow him. If he's going to his place, follow him there and park yourself in the bush. Rafe's got a spot for you. If Pollard's heading this way, follow. Make sure you have a good bead on him, in case he takes the Primrose Sands road along the coast.'

'Sure, got that.'

'And keep in constant radio contact. Faye, you do Ho's place. There's good parking along Sandy Bay Road. Use the car with the reflective windows. And Rafe, you keep tabs on Club Chillax. Hedda and I will see what more we can dig up on them. What we dearly want is Pollard and Ho together again, or failing that for one of them to lead us to a location that might clue us in more. You'll do ten-hour shifts, starting right after this meeting, and I'll sort out night replacements.'

'Ten hours?' Rafe looks pained. 'No break?'

'Yes and no to those. Any other questions?'

He persists. 'You're wanting eyes on them at three in the morning sort of thing?'

'Yes. That is exactly what I want. It troubles you?'

'No, boss.'

'Any other questions?'

None. I wave them out. Excepting Hedda, my co-equal in this caper. We've work to do.

121

15

THE COLD FRONT IS BIG, OMINOUSLY DARK IN THE AFTERNOON SKY.
The outlines of the Wellington Range vanish inside snow clouds and
freezing rain descends at a sharp slant. But it's forecast to dump and lift,
with a stable high moving across over the next few days. The farmers will
appreciate the rain, the Ben Lomond ski operators the snow, and the
weekend will be a sunny seventeen degrees. Only in Tassie, eh?

Magnus rings. When can we have that drink or have I gone off the
grape and therefore withered from the vine of life? He's a funny old
bugger, Magnus, still got the dogged persistence of an old-time cop.
But he's right, I keep putting him off. The truth is I just don't feel up
to his company, because he's free and I'm not, and when we have that
bottle or four of good red he'll be reminding me of it every sip of the
way, even though, being a good bloke, he'll try not to rub it in. And
even though the TPF – with the then young and ambitious Walter
complicit – shafted him badly.

I put him off one more time. He accepts with grudging good humor
and I tell him, not the first time he's heard, how magnusnanimous he is.
Shortly after Hunt's forty-eight hours is up I'll know whether my own
career's headed for the exit sign. There's a lot riding on Stan Fortune's
miserable murder. Wrongly fingering Athol Burden, if that's what we've
done, will be incompetence. Knowing who the real villains are, without
being able to convict them, will be incompetence with a triple-A rating
and a call for heads, chiefly mine.

MY MOBILE HAS A CONVENTIONAL RINGING TONE. IT AMUSES SOME
people: what's that strange brr-brr sound? I could have chosen Bach,
Burl Ives, Barnsey, a randy possum or even a string of underwater
farts, but dull prickly old Pufferfish went for the sound of a ringing

telephone. At half past five on a freezing dark morning, I can live with that sound, dragging me up from the depths of yet another dream forever unremembered as it ghosts away, leaving me to blunt reality.

'Sorry to wake you Mr Heineken, but the Dunalley watch has just called in. Pollard's Prado has just gone through. Heading to Hobart at speed.'

I call Rafe, waking him. I tell him to wake Faye and Troy. I call Hedda.

THE DUNALLEY TAIL FALLS AWAY AT THE TASMAN BRIDGE, RAFE TAKING over. I'm in my office, fixing a percolated coffee. Hedda comes in. We had tried to arrange a sleepover last night, but she was called away and it didn't happen. It irked us both. Now, we're edgy, not directly at one another but at the state of things, at whatever might be about to happen and over which we have little control.

Rafe tails Pollard directly to Ho's Sandy Bay home.

'Wish we'd been allowed to listen in on them, boss.'

'Never mind that. Sit tight. Faye and Troy are on their way in a backup.'

'Will do. But mate, this early I smell serious mischief.'

'Pollard wasn't racing to return an overdue library book. He's still your tail. Faye and Troy will be on Ho.'

'And if they come out in one vehicle, boss?'

'Then they'll be the only two-tailed ratbags in town.'

HEDDA AND I WAIT IN MY OFFICE. SHE TURNS MOST OF HER BACK TO ME and reads the *Mercury*. I'd like to read the future in my coffee sludge. Rafe calls in shortly after 7.30. Ho and his passenger Pollard have entered Sandy Bay Road. They're in the late model Nissan 370Z Coupe, shiny yellow with black trim, a plump turbo-charged beast with fat wheels and plenty of grunt. Faye and Troy are in our unmarked grey Berlina with reflective windows and, even in the sparse pre-rush hour traffic, I've every confidence in them to do the job without arousing suspicion.

Ho drives through the CBD and uses the ABC roundabout to enter the Brooker Highway, the principal arterial route feeding out of Hobart through the northern suburbs. Interesting. Early start equals long voyage? Or an appointment to be kept? Or both? Past New Town,

Moonah, Glenorchy, Chigwell, Claremont. Ho's keeping obediently to the speed limit. If you're tailing, visibility on the Brooker's reasonably good and our two can afford to sit way back. And a hot yellow sports number sticks out, so if you think you might be followed you wouldn't drive such a car, would you? But I'm sure Mr Ho's $60,000 lookatmoi is a pleasure to drive, especially if you're above the law. Or perhaps it's a chest hair substitute.

If they veer right and cross the Bridgewater Bridge at Granton they'll surely be aiming for the Midland Highway, the island's highway spine to Launceston and then Devonport on the northern coast, gateway to Planet Earth. But they keep to the left of the River Derwent. It's what we wanted. To the background crunch of Hedda taking a relieved bite of a Fuji apple, I call Walter to give him the potentially breakthrough news. But he's not in yet. So I call Hunt, who is in, and tell him. That Ho and Pollard are headed for New Norfolk. After that riverside town the Lyell Highway winding through the World Heritage Area has but one end destination – Strahan.

Faye and Troy are in the lead car. In the unlikely event of out-of-vehicle contact being made with Ho and Pollard, Faye and Troy will pass off as just another couple, whereas Rafe is now known to Ho. Furthermore, they're dangerous, and for that reason I don't mind Troy Seedge being in the mix. Not that my two can't look after themselves and each other. But if isolated, tiny Strahan is to be the location to confront them, that's a worry. TPF personnel aren't exactly numerous west of Derwent Bridge and Frenchmans Cap.

The trip from Hobart to Strahan generally takes five plus hours and they've already knocked off one of these. Time is also against us now. Faye calls in to report they're through New Norfolk and driving at a fair clip west, towards Tarraleah. Delightful hop country if you're a tourist, not if you're tailing likely murderers. If Ho and Pollard reach Strahan by midday and make contact with Kelpie Rossiter, what do Rafe, Faye and Troy do? Without a warrant to arrest them, not much they can do other than follow and watch.

I look out my window, down at the grim, cold courtyard, up at the low, bruised sky. What if …?

I make a call to a sweet-voiced young receptionist in Strahan.

'Yes sir,' she says brightly. 'We do have a reservation for a Mr Ho, staying tonight and tomorrow night. Mr Ho has booked our executive two-roomed suite. Do you want to leave a message for him?'

'No. Do you know when he made the booking?'

'Bear with me, sir … on the seventeenth of August. He was actually staying in the suite at the time, also for two nights.'

'Thank you.'

Phone down, phone up. I call Hunt again.

'Franz, what can I do for you?'

'When I interviewed Jay Ho he told me he never goes near the west coast. Well, he's booked into a waterfront suite tonight and he also stayed in it about forty-eight hours before Fortune was murdered.'

'That's what you've been looking for. Now you've got your reasonable grounds.'

'I certainly have, Grif. I want a warrant to enter his Sandy Bay property –'

Hedda bursts in, pointing two forefingers at me as if signalling a footy goal.

'You'll get it, Franz. I'll have it cleared ASAP.'

'Thanks Grif.'

Hedda's waiting impatiently. 'Unforseen circs, mate. The Lyell Highway's about to be closed at Derwent Bridge. Snow, ice, more on the way.'

We laugh at the sheer Tasmanianness of it. There's nothing unusual about the west being cut off in winter. It happens two or three times most years. The westies live with it, while tourists have their carefully scheduled itineraries thrown into chaos. We, the TPF, make the decision. Closures generally are anywhere from twelve to twenty-four hours. It means that our ratbags are not going to enjoy their waterfront suite tonight. But what does it mean for us?

I advise Rafe and Faye. The first radio announcement is due at the top of the ten o'clock news, and closure advisory signs are going up at New Norfolk and Hamilton. If Ho and Pollard have any brains they'll already have made enquiries about the state of the road. They also should have used Pollard's 4WD, because 4WDs are exempted from some closures. Perhaps our targets aren't too sharp on practicalities. Burying Fortune in a deer bag wasn't too sharp either, though to be fair to them they couldn't have anticipated a monster spring tide eating up their graveyard beach. The weather certainly hasn't been kind to them. Booking out the best suite in town wasn't bright either, though of course when Ho did that Fortune was alive and well and, presumably, not under threat. Which adds to our belief that it was a panic killing. And as they used to show us on the cop school blackboard in the old days, $M^1+P=M^2$, where M^1=Murder, P=Panic and M^2=Mistakes.

Faye calls in.

'Faye, what?'

'They can't have the radio on, sir. Unless they heard the news and are going to try to argue their way through.'

'They won't be the first. Okay, what's your Derwent Bridge ETA?'

'I'd say eleven. Maybe a bit longer if the Tarraleah bends are icy.'

'Keep in touch. And take care.'

16

CASE MOMENTUM IS A GOOD THING IN THIS BUSINESS, BECAUSE working in major crime is by definition a reactive process. To begin with, we always start third. The commission of the crime, followed by the discovery or reporting of the crime, brings us in. And often we're clueless. This is shaping as a classic case. An unidentifiable body and no weapon or motive morphed by degree into seemingly a kill-for-cash murder, a panicked rather than premeditated job, with an interstate bikie gang twist, producing a suspect who ticked all of Walter's boxes. But we hadn't, to use another of D'Hayt's charming phrases, worked ABCD – Above and Beyond the Call of Duty – on it, or perhaps it was just that impatience for a result got in the way. One million dollar's worth of cocaine, a dead gringo lookalike and three *autentico* villains later we do, at last, have momentum.

Hunt's lair. Self, Hedda, her boss John Petrie, Walter. It's midday and I have news for them.

'Go ahead, Franz.'

'Ho and Pollard arrived at Derwent Bridge at 11.45. They were strongly abusive to the uniforms at the roadblock. In fact, Rafe feared they might even try something on. Ho then made a call on his mobile and walked about in an agitated manner. That call lasted about three minutes. He then rejoined Pollard in the car. They sat in the car for a few minutes, presumably discussing the call and their options.

'Ho spoke again to our blokes at the roadblock, then he went into the hotel, returned to the car, and he and Pollard went back to the hotel, each with what seemed to be an overnight bag. They're now sitting in the hotel bar drinking. I can confirm that they've booked two rooms for the night.'

'That buys us some very useful time,' Hunt says. 'Is William Doll briefed and standing by?'

'He is. And I've sent a pair of techies to disable Ho's front gate system and house alarms.'

'What about Tredway, Addison and Seedge?' Walter asks. 'No way Tredway can show his face.'

'We've considered that. Addison and Seedge have booked into the hotel, posing as a couple. The place will get a sprinkling of stuck travellers, so they'll hopefully be able to keep an eye on Ho and Pollard. Tredway's got himself a Lake St Clair chalet.'

'Economy, I hope!' Walter means it as a joke, sort of, and there are chuckles, but I know my Tredway. He won't touch a drop of booze, but he'll monster whatever else is in the minibar and if he's got the option to score, say, a split-level room with spa and plasma screen, well, why not? How nice is that when it's minus two outside? As for Faye and Troy, they're in one of the world's unique establishments, a never-to-be-repeated mock Tudor pile in the middle of nowhere at the source of the River Derwent, namely Lake St Clair, Australia's deepest.

'And tomorrow, Franz?'

'I'd like to see what Ho's place might cough up before making that decision. As you say, Grif, we've got some time now. And momentum.'

IT'S A FAIR ASSUMPTION THAT HO WAS TALKING TO KELPIE ROSSITER before he and Pollard made the decision to book into the hotel. What we do know without any doubt is that Rossiter's cruiser, a Carver 530 Skylounge, still hasn't come through Hell's Gates into Macquarie Harbour, because Strahan's officers have been monitoring all vessel movements there, not difficult given that the channel's not much more than 100 metres wide. But he must surely be close.

I drive Hedda and William Doll to Ho's Sandy Bay place. A hidden plainclothes techie opens the gate, closes it smartly behind my Calais. The ripped-up bollards are still scattered at the top of the driveway. The second techie's waiting at the front door.

'I'll go and have a little look around,' Hedda says, once she's inside. She's got a good nose for where illicit substances tend to be secreted, and to that extent this job is a bonus for Drugs Branch, if they can finally pin Ho and his Club Chillax to the trade.

It was William Doll who had advised us on the likely physical circumstances of Fortune's death. Now, just inside Ho's front door, I present him with the likely location. He looks briefly around the portico, hops up the steps, walks the length of the passageway, returns to the steps. He briefly consults the autopsy folder. Confirming Fortune's weight and height, I reckon. Then he walks slowly down the steps and to the area of the portico where the outlines of stains on the stone slabs are faint, but, especially if you're looking for them, not all that faint. He puts down the folder and his black case, kneels. Closer and closer to the stone, which he sniffs. Then he stands and walks very slowly to the door and back to the foot of the steps, gazing down, wordless. Finally, he looks back up over the steps along the passageway. Imagining, like me, the last frantic dash of a doomed man.

'Well, Franz,' he says, 'there's no doubt that blood has been violently spilt here. I say violently because a formal bloodstain pattern analysis will confirm what my eyes are telling me, that these are significant and multiple types of bleed.' He kneels again, waves his fingers lightly over a patch of the floor, the stone appearing to be vaguely freckled. 'These are high velocity impact spatters, which can only have been induced by a gun. And see how they terminate in a straight line here. This, as you observed, is where the carpet ended.'

'I have to tell you, William, I'd only noticed those two larger stains.'

'Can't blame you.'

'They're passive?'

'Indeed they are. Typically, a heavy nosebleed or a deep cut from a knife or some such. Get down here, smell the detergent.'

I do, and can.

'And see those scrub marks, they're erratic, as if done in haste. Note also, Franz, how the passive stains are outlined. Thanks to our friends the erythrocytes. Oh yes, there was death here. But as you know, I have to prove that scientifically. Analysis of the blood scrapings I take will not be known until tomorrow afternoon, at the earliest.'

Doll sits on a step, opens his bag of tricks. I stand. Not used to going down on all fours. A good swim in the cold ocean would be nice. Get some of the rust out of the ageing bones. Erythrocytes make blood red. They produce the oxygen-carrying haemoglobins which give spilt blood its stickiness and which here, like a scum tide, will provide the damning DNA match with Fortune. Case solved. But it's far from over. There is the science. And the question, make that the problem, of Ho and Pollard, probably both armed, agitated, and soon to be hungover, in a hotel in World Heritage Area wilderness.

I think briefly of Athol Burden. I'm sorry for what he's been through. But if he helped lull Ho and co into a false sense of security, that's a fair return, though the nuggetty old son of the soil's profoundly unlikely to see it that way.

I walk into the lounge-room, into one, then another bedroom, four all up, each one huge. The place has high, elegantly plastered ceilings. I find Hedda in the billiards room.

'Check this out, mate. Bend down.' I do. Really getting old. Kneeling together under the billiard table, she pulls away a rug. Under it, flush with the floor in a neatly cut cavity, a small safe, locked.

'Cash, drugs, contact lists, something like that,' she says matter-of-factly. 'But I haven't actually found anything. So I'd like to get into this.' We stand, self feeling a tug in the lower back.

'It can wait. Doll's convinced they jobbed him there on the steps.'

'So how do we pick them up?'

'It won't be easy, but I think we should consider using the isolation of the west.'

'Stop them on the road?'

'Something like that. I'm also going to propose that you and I and a TROG take a chopper to Strahan. We need to know what's going on with Rossiter. As matters stand, he's an innocent party.'

'Who's budget is the chopper coming out of? You guys got six grand lying around?'

'My investigation so, yes, Walter's money.'

'He'll be thrilled with you. When do I pack?'

'I'd like us to be there this afternoon.'

'So we'll get to have that sleepover after all?'

'Looks like it, Andover.'

OUR TROG IS PAUL DE BRUYN, YOUNG AND GUNG-HO FOR A SPOT OF adventure. We take off from the Davey Street barracks in a Bell chopper, flip away from the city and rise quickly over the Wellington Range. The cultivated plains of the Derwent Valley soon enough give way to the uniform greens and iron greys of forests and mountains. Not so far below, the vast and black-dark lakes, Pedder and Gordon, with their myriad white spaghetti of hydro pipes, contrast starkly with the untouched wilderness from which they draw their energy. We're some way south of Derwent Bridge. The Franklin and Gordon look like dark motionless serpents in the dense green wilderness, which begins to drift in and out of vision as we move through low cloud.

Just before we took off I made final pre-flight contact with Faye. She reported that Ho and Pollard had eaten lunch and were continuing to drink in the great lounge of blazing fireplaces. They were getting pissed and seemed not to have their guards up. Ho had made another call, this one quite short, and signed off with a cheery laugh. Quite a few other patrons, she reported, had decided to dull the pain of the enforced stopover with drink. All in all, a party. I advised her of the finding at Ho's. That she, Troy and Rafe were watching over killers, confirmed.

17

WE TOUCH DOWN AT THE STRAHAN AIRSTRIP. IT'S COLD, WINDY AND raining fine sleet. The air smells of peat bog and buttongrass, the landscape scrubby and empty with a low horizon.

'Welcome to Strahan, Franz, Hedda, Paul.' Sergeant Ian Robins shakes our hands, and we walk at a clip towards his car. We bounce along the dirt road that takes us away from the airstrip and onto a slightly less bumpy dirt road. Robins turns right towards the coast.

'Show you where we're monitoring the Gates,' he says. 'I rounded up the Fitzpatrick brothers. Retired from the force, so I can trust 'em. They're doing twelve hour shifts.'

'I'm impressed, Ian.'

'Out here, Franz, we're masters of improvisation. We supplied most of this island's wealth, but you bastards from the east don't give a toss.' It's good natured. Or is it?

We speed along to the sprawling campsite of mostly green shacks hidden in the dense coastal vegetation and on to where the road tapers out and the forbidding granite chimneys of Hell's Gates appear, smashed by foaming white breakers which make the lighthouse almost disappear. The brothers Fitzpatrick have rigged themselves up a flash surveillance post. Backed well into a narrow gap in tall scrub is a Ford Raptor. Flask coffee, sandwiches and jelly beans on the passenger seat, a paperback novel, mobile and walkie-talkie at the ready. It's mid-afternoon, and this windy promontory of freezing rain and poor visibility is about as bleak a place as you could wish to be. Small wonder Van Diemen's Land's convicts decided they were entering hell when they passed through the narrow channel into the vastness of Macquarie Harbour, empty and featureless but for the prettily named Sarah Island.

STRAHAN HAS A POPULATION OF ABOUT 600. THE ONE-STREET waterfront has a jetty, a pub, and low clusters of tourist accommodation. You can explore the history of Huon pine. Rug up in the evening and watch a two-man play. Around a tannin-stained, waveless waterfront numerous small jetties jut from their owners' weatherboard or fibro homes. One of these jetties is sturdily built and longer than most, with a dogleg.

'Kelpie Rossiter's jetty. It reaches a channel, to take his boat. And that's his place with the deck. No need to worry about the missus, she'll be in her hairdressing salon in Queenstown.' Rossiter's house is double storey, not ostentatious, just bigger than everyone else's and with a deck running the length of the place, almost hanging over the narrow bitumen strip opposite his jetty and a forlorn-looking breezeblock public toilet. Robinson drives slowly, so we can take in the scene. This place is like a ghost town, but for a couple of chimneys pushing ragged lines of smoke up into the drizzle.

'You've had no hint of trouble from him?'

'None whatsoever mate. He's just another westie with lots of money, no hard questions asked about where it came from. He socialises in the pub now and again, takes his clients on fishing expeditions, and has a reputation for rooting anything with tits, oh, beg pardon.'

Hedda's heard it all before. She says, 'Then he's going to do it tough behind bars.'

'Want me to go around again, Franz?'

'No. Take us to where we're staying. I want a coffee and we need to work on likely scenarios.'

BY NIGHTFALL, WITH THE STRAHAN WATERFRONT BEGUILINGLY LIT up, its big Gordon River cruisers moored, one thing is clear. Ho and Pollard are well tanked and won't be slipping off anywhere under cover of darkness. I've raised the possibility of arresting them later tonight once they're conked out in their rooms back there in Derwent Bridge. But Hunt won't move until those spatters are proved to be human blood, and Fortune's. I have two TROGs under my command, and with Rafe, Hedda, Faye and six west coast officers we're surely very well equipped to deal with whatever might eventuate. But Hunt does say he'll be prepared to airlift a squad, should the situation call for it. So we wait.

We enjoy a feed in a Strahan pub, after which Paul de Bruyn excuses himself. He wants to clean his MP5 and Glock while watching something on TV. Fair enough. Hedda suggests a walk around to the old Abt steam railway shed. Ducks sit in the light-reflected water below the shiny hulks of the river cruisers. It's very dark ahead. Her idea of a walk is more like a stride in the inky blackness. Stars have begun to emerge. That means no more snow and that, in turn, means the road is likely to be re-opened once the ice has thawed a bit. Say ten am. So we can expect our ratbags around midday. High noon in the west. It can't come soon enough for any of us. I don't mind a little tension, but I'm feeling this in a way I haven't experienced for a long time. Can't put it down to age, because Hedda's pretty wound up too, not that she'd admit that. Not that I'd ask. We'd both like this to be the postponed sleepover, but that can't be, alas. It will just have to stay on hold. What I need now is some decent sleep. If not, Pufferfish will be an unacceptably growly DI come tomorrow.

'HEINEKEN.'

I'm yanked from deep sleep by the mobile. The luminous bedside clock reads 5.45 am.

'Ian Robinson, mate. Rossiter's Skylounge has just slipped in through Hell's Gates. She'll be at her mooring in about fifteen minutes.'

'Okay, we'll be out the front.'

I wake Hedda, then Paul, Rafe and Faye.

Robinson and a colleague in a second car draw up and we pile in, U-turn in the darkness and head for Rossiter's jetty. Paul de Bruyn's in full black combat gear. Rules of TROG engagement are super strict, with good reason, but he's an important element here because we're going to surprise Rossiter, and as a suspect in a murder case our tough little bloke will need to be discouraged from trying anything rash. An armed-up TROG all in black should do the trick.

We park some way from the jetty, move smartly forward. Robinson and his colleague will detain Rossiter's de facto to prevent her communicating with any third party. They cross the road. We wait against the breezeblock wall of the public toilet.

The wait begins to stretch and I'm starting to fear a problem when there's a sudden low pitch, very low but increasing, and the tall, shapely craft ghosts into view through freezing fog. Its cabin light is on, ditto the prow light, and we can clearly see Rossiter at the wheel. The vessel reaches the jetty, motors reverse thrusting as he expertly brings it alongside, chucks both mooring ropes around the jetty bollards, kills the motor.

The boat's about twenty metres away, bobbing gently in its own swell, marine diesel cutting sharply through the still air. Rossiter's whistling softly, a passable 'Stairway to Heaven'.

We wait while he comes and goes, tidying up the wheelhouse, stashing gear in the stern hatch, disappearing below deck, back up again, the peculiar little noise of his whistling intermittently floating to us over the flat water. Come on, Kelpie, come on. And at last he locks the cabin, hops lightly onto the jetty, a swag over one shoulder.

He must be wearing sneakers because his tread on the lit-up jetty boards is silent. He's wearing jeans and a wet-weather slicker. No longer whistling. I hold up one finger for de Bruyn and Hedda – ready to go.

The long hair's matted, shit-looking, ditto the beard. He sees me as I move, then there are three of us and I'm on the jetty, blocking his path.

'Kelpie Rossiter? Police. You're under arrest. Put the bag down.'

'What the fuck's this?'

Paul de Bruyn steps forward, stands alongside me, his MP5 pointed at the boards, but ready to lift. Rossiter eases the bag from his shoulder and lets it slip to the jetty.

'Let's go back to your boat, Mr Rossiter.'

He doesn't move. He puts his hands out. 'Guys, what are you doing? I'm a fisherman. I been fishing.'

'Let's go, please. To the boat.'

But he doesn't move, says, 'This is bullshit.'

'I remind you that you are not obliged to say anything unless you wish to do so, but whatever you say or do will be recorded and may be given in evidence. Do you understand that?'

It's now naturally light enough for me to see his eyes darting between the three of us, the fear in them.

'What the hell am I supposed to have done?'

'We have good reason to believe you're complicit in the murder of Stan Fortune.'

He shakes his head as if he's just been whacked a good one, like a solid rabbit punch. 'Mate! I been at sea for three weeks!'

'Onto the boat.'

He leads the way. Hedda has a quick look in his discarded bag. We step aboard, he unlocks the cabin, turns again to face us. 'This is crazy,' he says.

'When last were you in touch with Jay Ho, Mr Rossiter?'

'Uh ... jeez ... ages ago, mate.'

When in doubt, bullshit.

'What about Rob Pollard?'

'Same. I haven't seen 'em for years. Why?'

Answering a question with a question is seldom a good tactic.

'And Stan Fortune?'

Rossiter finds it in himself to laugh. 'Stan! He moved interstate when we were still nointers, mate!'

Finding something to laugh about in a situation like this is seldom advisable.

'So exactly how long have you been at sea, then?'

'Like I say, it'd be near three weeks.'

Hedda excuses herself past him and disappears below deck. He doesn't like it.

'And you were fishing?'

'Yeah, and looking for marlin.'

'Where?'

'Eastern seaboard. Port Stephens, Cairns, up and down.'

'So where are all the marlin, then?'

'No, mate, I don't keep 'em. I'm sussing out where they're running. I take clients marlin fishing. And tuna fishing.'

'Where do you do that?'

He looks at me as if I'm a bit thick. 'Out beyond Eaglehawk Neck.'

'The Tasman Peninsula.'

'Yeah.'

'You were down that way this time?'

'No.'

'Sure?'

'Totally positive, mate.'

Hedda returns, saying nothing. Rossiter looks at her. She holds up a small plastic envelope. Marijuana.

'Rec. use,' he says. 'Jesus, pointing that flipping gun at me 'cause I like a toke?'

I take a little wander, allow him to think about things. I open up the freezer hatch, peer in. It's quite full, and I raise my eyebrows at him, impressed, drop the lid. It bangs heavily. I wander back towards him. 'So Kelpie, if your mobile rings and it's Jay or Rob, that will be a pretty amazing coincidence, won't it?'

Even behind the beard, I can see his scrawny throat working. Paul de Bruyn hasn't moved all the while, boots planted slightly apart, the gun pointed at the deck, ready to lift. Call it 'overkill', eh, but the young TROG's presence is having its effect. Again, I take a little stroll. Towards the stern.

'Why should they call me?'

'Do you know that Stan Fortune died recently?'

'Uh … how should I know that?'

'True. If you don't listen to the radio at sea. Where did you say you've been? Off Cairns?'

'Yeah.'

I open the freezer hatch again. Rossiter and Hedda are watching me. Paul's watching Rossiter. A glimmer of weak morning sunshine suddenly bathes the deck pale yellow. Hands in, I firmly grab and yank out by their tails two frozen fishes, nice sized at about five or six kilos, broad tails, large heads, pale silver bodies with just a tinge of mauve. It would be fair to say that Rossiter's expression is that of a stunned mullet. Which these are not.

'Well,' I say, 'you've got one fuck of a cast, Kelpie. These are WA Jewfish, dhufish if you prefer, or just plain old dhuies, found only in the waters of the Western Australian coast. As a fisherman you probably know that.'

He just stares at me, at them.

'And I bet you kept them because you know they taste pretty good, Kelpie. Two questions. Why were you in WA, and why have you been lying to me?'

'Mate, no … haven't been lying …'

'Kelpie, you'll get seven for trafficking, life for murder. Come out in seven, you might if you're lucky still look a little bit like a Hollywood extra, and all that that has done for you in the way of shagging rights, but double that term and you'll exeunt Risdon looking way more like a gentleman of the road, bent and buggered.'

He's thinking hard, saying nothing.

'Kelpie Rossiter, I'm charging you as an accessory to murder. DS Andover, cuff him.'

'*No!* You got it wrong! How could I have killed the bloke? I swear to you I was at sea!'

'You can help yourself by helping us. I'll make an accessory to murder rap stick to you if I have to, like Super Glue. Try me, Kelpie Rossiter.'

'Oh, mate, they didn't mean to actually knock him off.'

The pocket of his wet-weather slicker erupts in the tinny riff of a rock song.

'Don't answer it, Kelpie.'

He doesn't. We wait. After about a minute, it beeps. Text message.

'Give it to me, Kelpie.'

He hands me his mobile. I flip it open. Read the text message: *Sleeping one off hey lazy bastid call me road open soon.*

'It's from Jay Ho, Kelpie.'

Kelpie looks shattered. I flick through some of his old text messages to check his idiom and spelling, then I send Ho a reply: *everythin sweet boys i just got in ill be waitin at home.*

'If he calls, Kelpie, we're not here, and you're happy.'

He swallows, nods.

There's soon a text reply: *onya kelps.* I text back: *goin to have a kip boys wake me when you get here.*

Rossiter slumps against the wheelhouse wall, exhales mightily.

'Are you prepared to make a formal statement about why and how Stan Fortune came to be killed?'

'Yeah. But I want a lawyer.'

'You do. As I say, Kelpie, you can help yourself here by not obstructing us in our duty. We know about the cocaine. We know that Fortune met his end in Jay Ho's house. All you have to do for us is join a few dots.'

'Mate, please, I had nothing to do with topping the bloke.'

'Join the dots, Kelpie. Why did they kill him?'

'He was an informant. They told me when I was two days out. We thought, what do we do? We reckoned, we've got the gear, Stan's dead, can't get worse, might as well still go with Plan A, sell the shit.'

'In Perth.'

'Yeah. I got contacts there. And to stay away from Sydney.'

'Good thinking, Kelpie. Nothing stirs a bikie like his powder once removed. Was it an accidental killing?'

'Yeah … I reckon.'

'Who pulled the trigger?'

'Mate, I was at sea. Jay told me they confronted him. He, I dunno, tried to do a runner. Then Jay just said the bloke died. We thought, what do we do? I was all for tossing the shit overboard and getting back in here.'

'You're just saying that, Kelpie.'

'No!'

'So you went to Perth and sold it, using your contacts there.'

'Yeah.'

'How much?'

'Quarter mil each. Stan … Stan just wanted … it was his peace offering to Rob.'

'Where's the money?'

'In a bilge tank,' Hedda says. 'In two oilskin bags.'

Kelpie Rossiter drops his head. He's fessed. Not that he had much choice. And the momentum is now unstoppable. The problem is how to stop Pollard and Ho.

THEY'RE PRETTY FLASH OUT HERE IN THE WEST. ROBINSON'S GOT A state-of-the-art video hook-up. Self, Hedda, Hunt, Petrie and Walter, the latter looking so close and real that I'm disappointed, confer on the best laid plan.

Hunt says, 'My overwhelming priority is public safety, so we'll let them leave Derwent Bridge.'

'We could lure them onto his boat,' Walter says.

'No.'

'Why not, Franz?'

'It's in the middle of a suburb, for Christ's sake. Do you want hostages? These are first degree killers with third degree hangovers.'

'What, then?'

'A safe trap. The Bradshaw Bridge at Lake Burbury. We have absolute control over it, in the middle of nowhere. We trap their car on the Bradshaw Bridge.'

'Tactical Response will have to decide on that, Franz,' Hunt says.

'No, Grif – I've decided. These maniacs are gunning a souped-up bumblebee at Queenstown and Strahan. I'm stopping them. With or without your last-minute helicopter load of TROGs.'

'Don't speak to me like that, Franz.'

'Sorry, Grif, but this has to be my call. It's too late to turn this into a TROG op, and there's no way I'm allowing those two through Queenstown and on to Strahan.'

Walter has to have his bob's worth. 'You're undermanned.'

'I have twelve armed officers, including the two TROGs. And every minute we argue is one lost.'

Hunt sighs. Silence. Then he says, 'What's your plan?'

'This is what I intend to do. First, traffic will be blocked from leaving Queenstown. We broadcast the reason as a small rockfall onto the highway. It's common enough. That will keep the Queenstown side of the road empty.

139

'At the bridge itself, at the Queenstown end, I want a mock roadworks set up. That will enable us to control the bridge at that end, close it off. And, of course, we'll be masquerading as roadworkers.

'The bridge is 350 metres long. By the time Ho is on the bridge and close enough to see that he can't get through, the bridge will have been blocked from behind.'

'How?'

'Rafe and Faye's vehicles. As well, I'll have a marked Queenstown car waiting in the scrub. It will drive onto the bridge and make the block total. I'll use a megaphone to get Ho and Pollard out of their vehicle. That, at any rate, is the plan.'

They digest it. Twelve versus two. Total element of surprise. No chance of public involvement.

'Okay,' Hunt says. 'It's authorised. But I'm choppering you backup all the same. I'll deliver ten armed officers into Queenstown. Can you arrange transport to get them to the bridge?'

'I can.'

'Good luck.'

KELPIE ROSSITER'S IN THE LOCKUP, DITTO HIS DE FACTO. THE DUTY constable's relieved them of their mobile phones.

Ian Robinson makes contact with his Queenstown counterpart to begin setting up the operation on the ground. The bridge is just twenty minutes from Queenie – up and over Mount Owen and down through the ghost hamlets of Gormanston and Lynda to the edge of the lake, the shoreline of which the road follows through exposed terrain for a few ks before reaching the long two-lane bridge.

We leave Strahan in a borrowed pool car. I'm mindful of black ice on the forest-shadowed road. Hedda's alongside me, de Bruyn in the back. Robinson and his constables follow. Rafe calls in from Derwent Bridge.

'When do you want the road opened, boss? Ho-ho-ho and Pollard are in pole position and looking none too good for wear, according to Faye.'

'A little while yet. I want the bridge set up exactly right first. They'll do the trip in less than an hour if Ho decides to test that machine of his. How many cars lined up?'

'Ten including us. Troy's driving he and Faye today because the road's sure to be iced and if Ho shoots off Troy's got way better road skills to keep pace with them. Me, I'm at the back of the queue such as it is so far, but that's no drama. Overtaking tourists on the bends of Mount Arrowsmith can only be fun.'

'Avoid the ravines mate,' Hedda advises.

Rafe, from his vehicle, is controlling the Derwent Bridge TPF officer at the closure barrier. It's just as well that Ho and Pollard are at the front. And in fact if they do go fast that will be good too, to put distance between them and the other travellers. I call Robinson.

'Ian, there's a chance that someone in a hurry could get caught up in this. I'd like to put one of yours in roadworker gear to operate a stop/slow sign. If he's placed a good one hundred metres before the bridge he'll be able to halt any following traffic.'

'Sounds good. Might help slow the suspects too, if you want that.'

'I'll advise Rafe and Faye.'

'Done, mate, leave it to me.'

Hedda glances at me. 'Talk about last-minute decisions.' She swings around, 'Anything you'd like to lob in, Paul?'

He laughs, says only, 'I'm ready.'

Hedda takes her Glock from her rib holster inside her leather jacket, checks the breech. 'Me too, I guess. And how about you, driver?'

'They've been interfering with my beauty sleep so, yes, I'm very ready.'

THE PLACE THEY CALL QUEENIE SPRAWLS ALONG THE QUEEN RIVER Valley, most of her few thousand souls engaged one way or another with the copper and gold mines of the region. And Queenstown is also that place of the psychedelic bare hills, long stripped of their vegetation by tree clearance for mine stopes and firewood, and then by acid rain from the mines. It pisses down here, up to three metres a year. And they play hard footy on a hard gravel oval. But we shoot through with our minds far from the quiet, neat streets and their quaint and tumbledown and sometimes damp-looking old buildings.

The road zigzags up the scarred ochre flank of Mount Owen, opening suddenly to a gigantic view of dark green wilderness with, far below, the shiny black length of Lake Burbury, a great manmade body of hydro water in the drowned Upper King River Valley. Beneath its waters lie the abandoned towns of Darwin and Crotty, forever drowned. At its southern end the lake empties into the King River, killed stone dead a hundred years ago by mine tailings. The distant pencil line of the

Bradshaw Bridge spans the lake at its narrowest point. For one arrested moment this peculiar landscape seems fitting territory for whatever is about to unfold.

WE DRIVE AT SPEED.

There's a pleasing degree of activity at this Queenstown end of the bridge. Two municipal trucks have been commandeered, their roadway signs strategically positioned. Robinson introduces us to his TPF colleagues. They seem ... what is it ... spring-stepped? They're defending their beloved patch from an eastern menace.

And now, driving slowly along the bridge, 40 kph signs in place at regular intervals, in the calm emptiness of this winter day I'm put in mind of the post-9/11 exercises we carry out each year somewhere in the island. But they are just that. Exercises.

At the far end of the bridge we get out again, look around. The TPF car is well back off the road, hidden from view unless you were looking for it. In the pale sunshine I brief the driver and the officer in reflective roadworker gear who may have to step out and operate the stop-slow sign. I don't want him exposed and I hope it doesn't come to that.

I head back to the car, taking in the scene at the distant Queenstown end. It's authentic enough. The roadwork trucks. The antlike figures in orange and yellow going about their business, a sense of work and smoko going easily hand in hand. I get back in the car. I pop the equivalent of a Pufferfish chill pill, a green, yellow, pink and black allsort. In front of us a clinking currawong bounces unconcerned across the bitumen.

'You can let them through now, Rafe.'

'TELL YOU WHAT,' HEDDA SAYS, 'DEALING WITH A ONE-OFF LIKE THIS IS the least of our problems.' We're in the car at the Queenstown end of the bridge, parked alongside the truck that's partly blocking one lane. 'Coke's flooding into Oz because the dealers have set up a two-tier market.'

'As in economy and luxury?' de Bruyn asks.

'Right. They've managed quite successfully, like working to a good business plan, to introduce heavily cut coke to the student and young party set, who aren't cashed up but want the glamour of being a cocaine user, like their movie and popstar heroes.'

'How cheap is cheap?'

'A gram of quality coke is about a hundred dollars, half that for a cut gram. And you can make your adulterated version go even further with polydrug behaviour i.e. cannabis, ecstasy, booze.'

Rafe calls in. 'Ho's flooring the pedal, boss, ice or no ice. I'm right up Troy and Faye's backside, pushing them, not that they seem to need the encouragement. We're sitting off about one k behind.'

'Where are you?'

'Collingwood Range. I'd say the Plain of Mists is somewhere about. Call you again in five.'

'Ta.' I relay the information to Robinson, who'll advise his troops.

Hedda laughs. 'My Troy-boy likes his cars fast and his guns noisy. Bet you're the same, Paul.'

'We have to be, to look after you guys. You're all soft.'

'Piss off, mate. But talking about ice, that's even more of a problem.'

'In what way?'

'Same principle. Economics. One kilo of coke equals one hectare of coca that has to be grown and then processed. Ice, on the other hand, can be put together in your kitchen. And is cheap as. About ten bucks a gram at the moment. The bikie gangs are starting to traffic the ingredients for that very reason.'

'A local rather than imported product.'

'You know it makes sense, as Sam Kekovich would say. Actually, this stoush between the Revs and Drags has probably got an ice connection, because traditionally ours has come from China via, y'know, Indonesia, Philippines, Burma.'

'And why is most speed made in Queensland?'

Rafe cuts in. '*Jesus Christ!* Ho's just about wiped them, they've skidded fifty metres, more …'

'Rafe?'

'Yeah, they're okay. Dickhead's slowed down. Guys, they were so close to being history, you have no idea.'

'Just you take care.'

'Will do, out.'

We contemplate it in the quiet morning.

'If Ho's a user,' Hedda says, 'and he's nursing a hard night I should think he'll have dropped a tab this morning and that won't be doing his sense of judgement any good.'

'Faye, Troy.'

'Boss?'

'You're well back?'

'We are, boss.'

'What about behind you, Rafe?'

'Yeah, a dickhead in a Beemer tried to keep pace, seemed to think it was fun, but not for long. Bloke must value his life.'

He must indeed. My calculation is that the following traffic, averaging about 60 ks in these conditions, will be a good fifteen minutes off the pace by the time the action gets underway. So in theory, by the time they arrive at the bridge it will all be over. In theory.

WE SIT IN SILENCE FOR A WHILE. I CATCH DE BRUYN'S EYE IN THE REAR view mirror. He's nervous. Time to talk.

'A final run through. If Ho obeys the 40 limit, they'll take about half a minute to drive the length of the bridge. Well before then, our vehicles at this end will have moved into their roadblock positions. By the time Ho and Pollard become aware that they're blocked off, they should be about two thirds of the way towards us, by which time Rafe, Faye and Troy will be on the bridge, with the marked car coming on behind them, the three of them forming the block at their end. I will get out and use the megaphone. Paul, you will get out and make it clear that you are armed. The marked cars at both ends will start using their lights, and that visual cue will hopefully persuade Ho and Pollard not to try anything stupid, though they're quite welcome to jump into the lake. Hedda, I'd like you to sit behind the wheel.'

'Sure.'

'Questions, Paul?'

'None. I work to standard operating procedure. I don't use my weapon unless it's to prevent them attempting to endanger life, including any attempt to take hostages. And, as far as possible, I take instructions from you as O-I-C on whether or not to use the weapon.'

'Good. I'll go and have a final word with Ian.'

When I return Hedda's in the driver's seat. I've tested the megaphone. Advised Hunt.

'Where are you, Rafe?'

'Into Victoria Pass. Road's straight as, he's pushing 130, and we can't afford to fall back now, we're too close to you guys. If they get suspicious it'll be now, because we're visible to them.'

'Hopefully they'll assume you're making up for lost time.'

'You better be right, boss.'

144

'Rafe, the final few ks after Nelson Valley, once you get your first sighting of the lake, are twisty, a down gradient. He'll have to slow for that. Don't endanger yourselves any further, do you understand? You're delivering them, we're dealing with them.'

'Copy. I'll advise Troy.'

'Call in as soon as you see the water.'

'Will do.'

WE WAIT. IT'S QUIET.

'Sighted the lake sir!'

'You're exactly two ks away.'

'Got that.'

'You're gonna cop us in a hurry, boss, we're *flying* mate!'

Rafe's so pumped I can almost smell it, or perhaps that's de Bruyn's acrid sweat. I hear him shifting his MP5 around. Easy, son.

'Rafe, we see them. Ian! Got a visual on the Nissan?'

'Got it, Franz, standing by.'

'Idiots,' Hedda mutters. A fine understatement. The Nissan whips through a dogleg, vanishes behind the treeline. I'm counting. Ten long seconds before Troy shoots through the dogleg at about the same speed, Rafe dangerously close behind Troy and Faye.

Have I done the wrong thing here?

Too late to consider that.

THE NISSAN CORNERS TIGHTLY AT THE BOAT RAMP AND CAMPSITE turnoff, in plain view now.

There's just one more sharp bend before the final straight approach to the bridge. We watch the vehicle slow into it, holding the road well. Ours have narrowed the gap. Looks like Troy's towing Rafe.

And now Ho and Pollard's compact yellow and black machine is dead ahead of us, descending rapidly to the bridge. The car slews slightly, braking hard, as it dodges past the roadmarking signboard and the 40 kph limit.

Onto the bridge. Still fast, but slowing considerably. Our two cars appear behind them.

'He's brake-dancing, boss. We've got the bastards.'

I wait until the Nissan is halfway across the bridge. Hedda's got the engine running.

'Go!'

We shoot forward past the truck, she swings the wheel, hits the brake, we slide a bit, come to an abrupt halt. Bridge closed.

The Nissan keeps coming. It's a hundred metres away. I hear the marked cars behind us, tyres squealing, sirens on, lights flashing in the rear view mirror.

I jump from the car with the megaphone, conscious of de Bruyn alongside.

The Nissan stops abruptly.

I bring up the megaphone, but needn't bother. The Nissan screams back to life, executing a wild three-point turn. Didn't they see they're trapped behind? Rubber smoke flares from the tyres.

'Let's go!' We leap back in, Hedda surges us forward.

Rafe and Troy have stopped their cars at parallel angles. Even so, there's a small gap. Too small for the Nissan, but it's aiming for them at high speed.

Rafe reverses wildly – he's aware of that gap.

I see, with dreadful clarity, Troy Seedge reaching around his driver's seat for his MP5, and as he tumbles from the vehicle in his haste the weapon skitters across the bitumen. He dives for it.

And then we see young Faye, out of the car, legs planted wide, her service revolver in both hands and she looks like she's just standing there, a statue, but the gun and her hands are bucking slightly, repeatedly.

The Nissan is surely going to hit them. But it swings violently, like a toy flicked by a child, and rams into the concrete side of the bridge, crumpling and scraping along in its momentum, screeching horribly, until it tips over itself and bounces to a halt on its roof.

Hedda hits the brakes. We spill out, run. The air stinks of smoke and burnt metal. Ho is jam along the barrier. Pollard's upper body hangs out of the bullet-shattered windscreen. Dark blood seeps from the lifeless head.

The silence is overwhelming.

Faye's hands, around her service revolver, slowly seem to be lowered by gravity. She bows her head.

Hedda holds her, hugs her, as sound and noise erupt everywhere.

18

THE THREE BELLS IS A PUB THAT CLAIMS TO HAVE BEEN SERVING alcohol and hospitality to Hobartians without interruption since 1836. I can't vouch for that. What I can vouch for is that its indoor man ferns – into the pot of one of which Rafe allegedly pissed recently, although it seems aeons ago – appear to be in the bloom of ferny health. And it's equally true that this has been the unofficial TPF watering hole for many a year. Which is why it was the location for an almighty Saturday evening party that went on into the small hours of this morning, celebrating what the media quickly and cutely dubbed 'The Bradshaw Bridge Ambush'.

As a cop you don't know when you'll be put through the mill. Rafe was. Troy was. We all were. But nothing remotely like Faye was. She killed two men. It's in her job description. What's not in that description is the emotional and psychological impact of such a deed. As a brutal lesson in mortality, it shocked all of us who were there to witness it and there's no knowing how she'll cope, or not cope. She'll get all the care and attention that she needs, or that we think she needs. She did seem to enjoy herself at the Three Bells, though she left early. She plans to be at work tomorrow and to give her evidence at the internal inquiry into the deaths. I'll be watching her carefully.

Just as I'm watching for more bloody black ice, this time on the road through Taroona on the western shore of the estuary, south of the city. It's shortly before eleven in the morning, my head's in a sorry state from far too much booze and too little sleep, but I'm off to have more. There must be something wrong with me, eh? I drive cautiously along the winding old highway, past the mighty old sandstone Shot Tower, the bitumen deep black and glistening. An inquiry into deaths caused by police is standard. What makes this different is the extent to which I may have placed my colleagues in harm's way. That I pressured Hunt and Walter who, not being on the scene, were all but obliged to agree to my plan. What else could or should have been done?

I'm sure to be asked why I didn't exercise more patience. That we could have allowed them to get together with Rossiter in Strahan, do their stuff, and then have the professionals, the TROGs, apprehend them at some ungodly hour of the night in their beds. Two speeds will save me there, that of the Nissan and the phial of pills and handguns retrieved from Ho's car. Alive and on the road he was a menace, a threat to the good folk of the west coast, end of story. What's most likely is that I'll be officially reprimanded for speaking abusively to Hunt, then he'll invite me up for a sherry and we'll go from there.

I park. It's a fine morning, a sky of such pale winter blue it might crack. The neatly mown grass at the front of his place is bright green. My head throbs. Too bad. No way I could have put him off again. I knock. He's at the door at once, the big, friendly ruddy face, jowls, close-shaved iron-grey head of hair, one eye milky-blue and staring, the one that hasn't worked since he got acid squirted in it a few years before they pushed him out of the TPF.

'Mate! Look at ya!'

'How are you, Magnus?'

We embrace lightly. He's grinning. 'Well done, you grumpy old Dutch son of a bitch. That's two less. Good work.'

'I've got such a filthy hangover I'm wondering if it was worth it.'

'Hair of the dog will see you right. How's the kid?'

'Too soon to tell. I think she'll be okay. She's …' I shrug.

'Yeah. We'll go straight over to Bendt's.' Magnus shoos his Manx cat back in, cheerfully slams his front door shut. 'Make sure they don't put too much of that new age shit in her head. She was doing her duty with all of you other fellas and the bad guys, armed and drugged up, got what they deserved. She was just the one behind the trigger. And you, mate? I heard you jumped in their path with a megaphone.'

'Not quite. Don't believe everything you read in the *Mercury*.'

He leads us along a narrow muddy path between his house and the high, thick yew hedge of a neighbouring property. Blackbirds, with their intense yellow beaks and bright brown eyes, flit in front of us, barely above the mud. 'Don't believe everything a cop tells you, either.'

He takes us through a latched gate set in the hedge and we emerge in the garden of a large, solid house, around which we walk to its front, onto a porch. Something vaguely familiar about this place. In thirty long years of being a cop, did I come here? No recollection. Must have …

148

Magnus's meaty hand grabs and whacks the big brass door knocker. 'Eagle', he says matter-of-factly.

I'm staring at that knocker. 'I thought it was a vulture.'

He gives me a mildly puzzled look. The door opens. Bendt is a little bloke, dapper, collar and tie, a kind of old fashioned smoking jacket.

'G'day, mate!' Magnus pumps Bendt's delicate-looking arm up and down. 'This is Franz Heineken, a good bloke. I was telling him all about you, Bendt.'

'Hello, Franz. You are in the news! Come in, come in.'

He's got a marked accent, Danish for sure. The lounge-room's even more familiar. What the hell's going on here? My brain can't be that dehydrated. I look at the neat rows of books in their floor to ceiling shelves. And there, that other room off to the side, with its double doors, what's up? …

'So, mate,' Magnus is saying, 'what Bendt here doesn't know about wine doesn't need to be known. Hey, Bendt? Am I right or am I right?' And Magnus laughs heartily, well pleased at having scored himself such a princely neighbour in the matter of the grape. And Bendt clearly likes the attention, in the way that a vintage car collector likes publicly displaying his vehicles.

'Franz,' Bendt says, as if making an announcement, 'I think we should celebrate your recent success in catching those crooks.' He grins. He has a gold rabbit tooth, goes well with his bright baby-blue eyes. He turns and walks to a bookshelf, at one end of which he removes a large tome from its place on the third from bottom shelf. He puts his hand in the space so created. I watch, amazed, as his finger pushes a button and the shelf begins to turn on its central axis, slowly revealing a hidden door. 'My wine cellar is this way,' Bendt says with calm pride. 'The architect, you know, escaped East Berlin in the 1950s and came to live here in Tasmania as a refugee. Perhaps he brought some of his paranoia with him? But it suits my purpose very well.'

Bendt politely gestures us to precede him into the cellar. I go first, down a ramp into a level space about three by four metres, and no more than two metres high. It's lit by two electric lights and two temperature control thermostats are set in the walls. The two walls themselves are neatly crammed with wine racks, and they're all full. I'm astounded. I turn. Magnus is looking expectantly at me. Little Bendt, behind him, peeks around him at me.

'Did he build any other houses here like this?'

'Yes,' Bendt says. 'A couple, I believe.'

'Do you know where?'

'There is one up the mountain. Somewhere near Fern Tree. Not that I have seen it.'

But I have.

ANOTHER THING ABOUT COPPERY IS ITS RELENTLESSNESS. THINGS happen. You can't just switch off. I hoot impatiently outside Rafe's West Hobart place. Even though I rang him half an hour ago, he's obviously not ready. It's just after two in the afternoon. Finally he comes out. In one paw, a chocolate milk, the working class beverage of choice after a big night. He looks terrible, even behind impenetrably dark shades. Slept-on unwashed hair, unironed shirt, tradie's crack, his daggy, too-tight bomber jacket and filthy old Blunnies.

He groans into the passenger seat, fumbles for his seat belt with what looks like a shaking hand. 'For Christ's sake, boss.' His voice is rough. 'I only got to bed at eight this morning.'

'You pissed it up all night?'

'Well, we stopped for a bit. Had a feed at Sandy Bay Maccas then kicked on to the Gen Zed Club.'

'Big mistake.'

'Tell me about it,' he mumbles, has a suck on the milk. 'Mate, this had better be good or the payback will be long and terrifying.'

'It'll be good, Detective Tredway, it'll be good.'

'Why're you being so secretive anyway? And how come you're bright as a button? You were pretty pissed last night, you know.'

'I've found that the Grange Hermitage '71 is an excellent cure for a hangover. You should try it sometime.'

WE TURN OFF FERN TREE ROAD, BEYOND THE PUB. I DRIVE SLOWLY UP the long winding driveway. The Kia's there. As is the pair of hefty stone kneeling hyenas flanking the porch pillars.

This time I use the eagle head. Three sonorous bangs. Cristobel da Souza opens the door.

'Yes?'

'Good afternoon Cristobel. We need to come in please.'

'Is Mr Collins-Bower expecting you?'

'No.'

She hesitates, then steps back. We file past her, into his lounge-room.

Warwick Collins-Bower wheels himself from his museum annexe. Takes us in.

'Gentlemen, what do you want now, for goodness sake? I was about to nap.'

'Mr Collins-Bower, I have reason to believe that you may have kept information from us in relation to the disappearance of your wife, Virginia.'

He glares at me. 'We've been through all of this!'

'Not quite.' I walk to the bookshelf, remove a book from the third from bottom shelf.

'*Hey!*' He bellows at me, furiously wheels himself towards me. Cristobel half-heartedly steps forward. Rafe puts himself in the wheelchair's path.

I push the button firmly. The bookshelf swings slowly on its axis.

'*Oh meu Deus!*' Cristobel's hand clamps over her mouth. Rafe has to grab the wheelchair to prevent the old man driving himself into me and he jabs a finger down at the enraged old face.

'Mate, I'm doing you for attempted assault on a police officer.'

That's unusual, I admit, but nothing like what I now encounter. In the vaguely aromatic darkness I feel for and find the light switch, walk down the ramp. In this vault, not wine racks but a fold-up camp table. Nothing on it. But it's surface is stained, and filmed with an off-white dusty substance. At each end of the vault there are large bar heaters. They'd keep the room nice and warm. And neatly lined up on the floor, piles of evidence. He must have got lazy, or even forgotten about them. Empty bottles for a start, their labels identifying them as pistacia tree resin, frankincense, myrrh. There are screwed up balls and empty rolls of cling wrap.

I've seen enough. Did he do it alone? It's just possible. The fact is, he did do it. He took revenge against his wife, Virginia, for sleeping with his colleague and giving away his breakthrough knowledge of the Meroitic script, all those decades ago in Pomland. I fold my arms, consider this eerie crime scene.

If acting alone, I reckon he poisoned her, then managed to put her body across his lap, wheeled her in here, laid her out on the table. He would have used some kind of sharp-edged hammer to smack the top of her nose, breaking the ethmoid bone. Then he stuck a thin, hook-ended rod up the nose, pushing it through the broken bone into her brain. Then he would have spent some time twirling the rod, pulping up the brain and reducing it to mush. Wonder what would have been on his mind at the time? The ancient Egyptians didn't think much of the brain, apparently. They were big on hearts, though. Bit of effort for Mr Collins-Bower now, turning his Virginia over to enable the brain liquid to seep out through her nostrils. I should think the hooked rod is in the museum annexe. In fact I remember seeing it on my last visit here. Not that I thought at the time that he'd be the type to pour pistacia tree resin into his wife's empty brain socket to clean it.

And that done, he would have removed her eyes and then made a generous cut on the left side of her body and taken out the innards – the liver, lungs, stomach, intestines heart. In their place, packets of natron, stuffed into the cavity to do their thing. As an Egyptologist of renown, he'd have had a legitimate stash of the stuff, its sodium carbonate component absorbing the body's liquids and its sodium bicarbonate component waging war on any bacteria silly enough to interfere with the process. The ancient Egyptians knew how to do life after death, all right. Then again, no more complex than skinning and mounting a stag deer. Collins-Bower would then have covered the body and innards with natron, and wheeled himself out of here for about five weeks.

He returned to a shrunken body, about seventy-five per cent of it having been absorbed into the natron. The childlike frame must have impressed him. He obviously stuck to the script, cleaning the body with frankincense and myrrh and oiling it to keep the skin from cracking. The dehydrated internals would have been popped back in the cavity. Not sure about the eyes. An unusual aperitif, perhaps. No embalming linen for Warwick, though. Cling wrap is much quicker and just as effective, in the way that ageless, mummified Vladimir Lenin is encased in a film of invisible rubber. Forensically, this is a bigger gold mine than any found on the west coast of Tasmania. But where's the body?

In the lounge-room the three of them are like extras on a movie set, waiting for my return and instructions for the next take. Rafe's standing over the wheelchair. Cristobel da Souza has mascara tear lines down her cheeks. And Warwick Collins-Bower also looks like he's had the liquid sucked from him, so shrunken and vapid is he now, so pasty grey-skinned.

You don't have to be a rocket scientist to be a cop. It may come in handy once we inhabit distant galaxies, but not now. I have added two and two and I have one simple instruction.

'Would you open that sarcophagus again, please, Rafe?'

'Sure.' He walks into the museum annexe.

He can't be all that sure, because he hasn't seen what I just have, and he opened it less than a month ago. But the enigmatic Pufferfish has told him to, by way of asking him to.

Rafe walks into the museum annexe, to the standing wooden box of the female thousands of years old, her golden face with arms crossed over her chest, her mane of big black-and gold striped hair. I stand in Rafe's place, guardian over the wizened Collins-Bower.

In his familiarity with it Rafe takes a wide-legged stance, grips the sarcophagus bodily, lowers it carefully on its side to the floor, humphing a little at the effort. He drops to one knee to pop its clasps, stops abruptly.

'Boss, there are new screws in here.'

'Open it, Rafe.'

From his bomber jacket, it's definitely too small, must tell Faye to inject some kind of dress sense into him, he palms what we ironically like to call the Tasmanian Air Force Knife, a high-quality, green and yellow local version of the Swiss original.

The click of the miniature screwdriving implement in his big hand couldn't be louder. From the hidden cellar, light aromatic wafts. Herbs, dry saltiness, afterlife.

My Detective Tredway brooks no shit. Works the screws out fast, pops the original hinges. Lid up, his face in. Rears back and away, as if struck.

I don't know if inhaling fresh mummy is a more effective cure for a hangover than Grange Hermitage '71, but judging by Rafe's expression it is.

'Boss … Jesus … Come and look at this.'

I do. A spice- and oil-preserved cadaver. Shiny awkward brown, skin like kinder paper to draw happy things on. No eyes. Maybe he enjoyed them with a cleansing vodka chaser. A small, dehydrated reminder that we are nothing.

IS THERE A LORD GOD? PERSONALLY, I HAVE MY DOUBTS. CONTEMPLATING God is big business. But I could be wrong. I've been wrong before, any number of times, and muddle-headed into the bargain. I'm an old, granite cop. Now, back at my Bruny Island shack for just one night, the one I should not have been allowed to have. Stroked by happiness. I swim out to the sacred rock, freezing saltwater stripping rust from my old bones.

I stand on the rock, shivering in pathetic sunshine. Looking out.

Her kayak materialises, a slip of orange splinter in the estuary, coming this way. She'll be here in twenty minutes. Time to boil that cray. Time to open that French red, courtesy Bendt, pressed on me by Magnus. They say a wine of such stature needs to do some serious breathing once the cork's out. And who am I to argue?

DAVID OWEN

How the Dead See

A PUFFERFISH MYSTERY

SHARK

In peril in the sea

Second Revised Edition

DAVID OWEN

Milton Keynes UK
Ingram Content Group UK Ltd.
UKHW020750051024
449151UK00011B/502